Happy Reading!

#Hipster

Dedication:

To every hipster who hates hipsters.

Printed in the United States of America

First Paperback Edition published, June 2018

This is a work of fiction. Names, characters, places, and incidents either are the products of the author's imagination or are used fictitiously. Any resemblance to actual persons, living or dead, businesses, companies, events, or locales is entirely coincidental.

10 9 8 7 6 5 4 3 2 1

ISBN
9781070559391

#GroupProjectsTotesFML

Call me Rebel. Because, you know, that's my name. Rebel Young to be exact. I know. A bit on the nose, given my style and hobbies. I think that's because my parents knew I wasn't going to go with the grain of society, even as a baby. I'm different. And I'm proud of that, as everyone should be. If everyone is supposed to be unique, why would you strive to be normal? That just didn't make any sense. I embraced my differences whole-heartedly. Hell, I strived to be more different than my bourgie family even tried to be. And trust me, that's saying something. But I'm sidetracking.

The point is, I'm different. Because I'm different, I look at things differently. I've always been the one my friends go to for fresh advice on the world, solicited or not.

I walked down the main street of VCU campus (Virginia Commonwealth University in the small "city" of Richmond, Virginia, for those of us in the know), sipping on my double tall pumpkin spice mocha latte and off to my favorite college class of the semester, Internet Writing. Pretty much in this class, we studied memes and how they catch on so quickly in society. It's cool seeing how trends piggyback each other into something new. We even learned where the word "meme" comes from. Did you know that it actually came from the genetics term "mimetics," derived from the Greek word "mimema," which roughly means "that which imitates or copies"? See? And you just thought it meant a popular joke online. You learn something new every day.

Anyway, I'm a creative writing major with a minor in philosophy. I know, people always say that liberal arts degrees won't get me a job, but what do they know? My sister, Lucy, was an economics major with a minor in business, a degree everyone preaches will guarantee earn you a job once you turn the tassel on your graduation cap. And yet, she still doesn't have a job after she graduated a year ago. So, knowing I'm not getting a job out of college anyway, I'd rather pursue my passion than struggle in a major I don't get or believe in because it looks better on a resume.

The campus was alive and thrumming with the sounds of students lively chatting, and the birds chirping. The fall air was brisk and fresh, and the wind sweeping through the campus ran its fingers through my black hair with rainbow colored tips. I dyed it specially that way after I saw it pinned on my Pinterest wall. My newly polished fingertips (yet, already chipping! How does that happen!?) had to keep my black wide brim hat from flying off my head to dance with the wind.

I checked my phone as I walked, hoping to find a couple more likes or retweets on my tweet from the campus Starbucks, "@starbuckscoffee: getting a pumpkin spice latte before class! #totesdelish, #skoolzhard, #PUMPKIIIINSPIIICE." Yeah, I made that last one up, but I'm sure it'll catch on. Like "Fetch." And hey, look a new follower!

I downed my drink and tossed it in the recycle bin outside before I entered the computer lab where the class is held. I logged in and pulled up my blog for the class and read over my homework. I usually wrote poems about cute pictures I found on Instagram every week. This week's post was about a couple kissing in the rain under a red umbrella. #TotesAdorbs.

The class filled in slowly, everyone taking their seats at their respective computers. Our professor, Ms. Alma Harris, waltzed in taking her place in front of the projection screen and smiled. I always loved her style.

Her blonde frizzy hair was tied back in a bun, with wisps of it haloing her face. Her lips were painted a bright red, making her fifty-something year old smile look younger. Her brown horn-rimmed glasses hung around her neck over her black turtleneck. She also wore black skinny jeans and brown suede ankle-boots. Her one pop of color was her red and brown geometrically designed wool poncho, which accentuated her thin frame.

"Welcome back, class," she greeted with a smile. "Now, I saw all your posts for the weekend, and I've got to say your posts this semester have been top notch. But I'm sorry to say, this weekend was the last post you'd be making on your blogs."

My heart froze. *Last post?* Why would she be cancelling our normal homework?

"Since it's November, and almost the end of the semester," she added the second part almost begrudgingly, "we are going to start the final group project with one of, probably, the most important internet contributions to the writing world, National Novel Writing Month, or more commonly known as NaNoWriMo."

Suddenly, I was excited ... and nervous ... and not really listening to Ms. Harris explain the origins of

NaNoWriMo, or its significance in the writing community. I knew some of it already. Well, not how it started, but I knew the effect it had on publication and the publishing process. But what was more important was I had never written a novel before. Actually, I doubt anyone in my class had written a novel before. But, in all honesty, which I would *never* admit out loud, I hadn't really written a story either. I mean, I had plans for stories, but my work always turned out more poetic than prose. But *group project*? How was that going to work?

"Over the past couple months, I've been reading your posts, and I've set up groups based on your writing styles," Ms. Harris explained, opening her teacher's notebook. "Now you will be in groups of three or two, with a total of five groups in the class. What everyone will do is once you hear your assigned group, I want you all to join each other and discuss your novel for the rest of the class period. Ready?" We eagerly nodded. She whipped out her list and began reading. The other students began standing up when their names were called and congregating in different corners of the room.

"Group Four: Rebel Young." I beamed as I stood up, eager to find my partner. "And Mike Davis." My good mood and excitement instantly drained, and the room's volume notably went silent. And here I thought my multicolor pastel nail polish chipping this morning was going to be the bane of my day today. Thanks Ms. Harris for proving me wrong. I turned to see Mike sitting in the corner, a sardonic smile on his face as he shook his head.

How could I describe Mike? Vanilla? Yeah, vanilla. He was cookie-cutter vanilla. He was your standard frat guy, aka "Skittle Shirts," as my friend Aimee and I liked to call them. He regularly wore standard jeans, a polo, and Sparries. I'd give him credit for not popping his collar, but still. His light brown hair was short and had no sense of identity. It looked like he went to the barber with one of his frat bros, pointed to his friend's head, and said "I want that." Remember when I said, "If everyone is supposed to be unique, why would you strive to be normal?" Yeah. He was the guy striving to be normal. Again, I don't get it.

The only standout feature he had were his bright green eyes that seemed to hold back a biting wit. A biting wit that I had been on the receiving end the previous semester in our Intro to Creative Writing class in the Spring. A class half of our current classmates were in with us. And who had all witnessed the verbal shit-storm and breakdown that sprung from that biting witty critique he made about one of my pieces. I was an artist! Who was he to say I had no sense of creative writing?

Slowly, I grabbed my things and made my way over to his spot as our professor continued calling out the last team. I plopped my notebook and purse in the chair next to him, sitting down with a huff. My tongue rubbed against the cold metal of my lip ring, a habit I picked up not long after I got the piercing.

His smile was pearly white as he said, "Hello to you, too."

I only graced him with a small, "Ugh."

"Alright, class. Begin," Ms. Harris called out.

As the class began the slowly increasing volume of noise that came along with class discussion, I remained notably silent, picking at the dirt under my nails. There was no point on getting started on an assignment that I wouldn't be finishing. Definitely not with Mike.

"So," he started, tapping the eraser of his pencil on his open notebook, "what are we going to write about?"

"*We* aren't writing about anything," I snipped back, crossing my arms and giving him a scathing look. "I am talking to the professor to get switched out of this group." She was one of my favorite professors, always complimenting my posts and work. If she knew how much we hated each other, she surely wouldn't force us to work together for a whole month.

His green eyes shone with an evil delight before he said, "Well, you better think of a quick argument, because she's on her way over here."

The hairs on my neck stood on end as I heard Ms. Harris step up behind me and ask, "So, are there any ideas being tossed around?"

"Well, Rebel had an idea," he said sarcastically, holding up an offering hand as he gave me the floor. That evil little glimmer in those green eyes shone a little brighter with glee. What a jerk.

I shot him a short glare before turning and smiling at our professor. "Yeah, see. I don't think our group is going to work. We," I gestured between Mike and I, "kind of hate each other."

Ms. Harris smiled. "I know."

My smile fell a little. "You know."

Ms. Harris nodded sagely. "There's a reason I put you two together. You both are my top students, and I realized that you each push each other as rivals to do better. I wanted to harness that potential in this project," she explained.

My smile was forced now. "Right."

"Now," Ms. Harris continued, "if you don't want to work with him, that's fine. But I will have to give you a zero on the project if you don't actually work together."

"Right," I repeated, my gaze drifting to an ancient stain in the middle of the floor.

"What about you, Mike? Do you want to switch?" Ms. Harris's gaze switched to Mike's, and it was clear that it was a challenge. One that no student in their right mind would try.

"No, Ms. Harris. I'm good," he replied in an almost jovial voice.

"Good, get to work."

I refused to look at anyone as Ms. Harris walked away. There was a soda stain on the carpet. It looked old. I focused on that, finding it easier to muse how someone broke the one computer lab rule than face the reality that I had to work with a jerk like Mike.

"So," I heard him start again, sounding so smug, "what are we writing?" I clenched my fist I tried to let out a calming breath, something I learned in my Zen Yoga class two semesters ago. I'm not normally the violent type, but it was taking a lot of restraint to not punch him in the face.

"Come on, Rebel," Mike grumbled into his notebook on the desk. "We have to settle on a topic to write on."

"I said a dystopian romance," I replied nonchalantly. An hour had gone by, our classmates had left with their novel plans fifteen minutes ago, and he and I still sat there with not even a theme for our book.

"No!" he groaned, not lifting his head. "Something easy that we can plan and crank out in a month. Something like a mystery."

I scoffed. "How do you know a dystopian romance wouldn't be easy?"

Mike finally lifted his head and gave me a long hard stare. He narrowed his eyes as he hissed, "Fine. Since dystopian romances are 'easy,' according to you, what's the plot?"

I stopped in in my tracks. "Plot?" Always my soft spot when it came to writing. Of course he knew that from our previous class together. Now he was just trying to goad me.

"Yeah," he growled back. "Who are our star-crossed lovers? How does their love transcend and expose this dystopian society? How do they realize they love each other?"

"Uhm," I stammered, "I don't know." He groaned, dropping his head in his hands. "Well, *yet!* We just got the genre!"

"A genre means nothing without a plot!" he snapped back. "Hell, a book is nothing without a plot!"

"Well, then, help me!" I fired back. "I'm not the only one supposed to be working on this!"

"I would help you, if you didn't *shoot down all my ideas.*"

His green glare pierced my own, causing my breath to catch in my chest. Maybe I was being a little bit one-sided and sore about working with him. I looked down at my hands, fiddling with an antique opal ring I had worn on my left index finger. It was my favorite thrift shop find. Mostly because it was so simple, and beautiful.

"Fine," I breathed. "What do you suggest?"

He leaned back in his chair with a huff. "Let's meet in the middle," he started. I frowned. *In the middle?* "You want to do a romance, fine. We'll do a romance as a sub-plot to a mystery or thriller novel."

I sank in my chair. I wasn't going to get to go into all of my descriptive writing like I'd want to in a mystery or thriller. And that was what I was good at. But I did have to admit he was right, as much as I hated it. This project was only lasting a month, and most authors couldn't produce a good manuscript for a novel until after a year.

"What do you say?"

I let out a long breath before I replied, "Mystery. Mystery and romance."

Finally, a relieved smile appeared on his face as he said, "Good. Now before we plan out the plot, is the romance a tragedy or not?"

I shrugged. "Why don't we see what the characters say?"

"No," he snapped, his pointed frown back. "That's not how authors write."

I frowned back at him. Now, I know that *that* was bullshit. Authors let the characters write their stories all the time. The good ones, at least. That's what every Hollywood and indie film about authors told me.

I crossed my arms, and snarked back, "Then how do authors write, Mr. Professional-Writer?"

"They make a plan. Every author worth their salt knows where the plot is going," he explained tiredly, rubbing the base of his temple. "It may be an abstract plan or incredibly detailed, but it's still a plan. So, again I ask, are we setting this romance up to fail or prosper?"

I narrowed my eyes at him before stating, "I don't think I *want* to write a romance with you."

That did it. He banged his head against the desk and groaned, "I swear to *God*, you are going to drive me insane!" Before I could make a snide comment back, he shot up from his chair and grabbed his things.

"Wh-what are you doing?"

"What's it look like?" he snapped back. "I'm leaving."

"B-but we haven't gotten a story figured out yet," I started, sounding a little lost, "or characters, or a schedule. Who's posting the first chapter? When?"

"Look, I'm leaving because you *clearly* don't want to work on this, and I refuse to sit here and do nothing except argue for another hour," he growled, slamming things in his army green and taupe satchel. "As far as a schedule and plot goes, I'll write up a plot and email it to you, as well as a schedule. Hell, I'll post the first chapter tonight." He ripped a page from his notebook and wrote down a number briskly, then slid the page over aggressively. "Text me your email."

Then he walked to the door, leaving me alone in the computer lab, and a little lost about what just happened. *Did he just say he's doing this alone?* I looked at the paper, which read "Mike Davis: 570-241-9960." I shot from my chair and almost ran after him. Luckily, he hadn't made it to the outside doors just yet when I called out to him. "Mike! You can't just leave!"

"See, that's where you're wrong," he replied, not even looking back at me as he pushed open the door, letting the chilly November air pass in through the hallway.

I huffed, and stomped my foot. I wasn't going to follow him out there. I didn't even have my jacket on. I stormed back into the computer lab, snatching up my things. I grabbed my phone and paused. Maybe I could have the last laugh. I typed his number in the top bar for contacts and picked my words carefully. *If you think that I'm just going to let you assume control of our project, you're dead wrong!* I hit send. I packed up my stuff in a flurry. Then let out a huff. How could someone be such an ass? I looked back at my phone. We do have to work together.

ry05796@vcu.edu I typed. I set my phone down and shook my head. What the hell was I getting myself into?

As I finished packing up my things, my phone buzzed against the desk. I frowned as I picked it up, and swiped it unlocked.

K. Thx.

K? Is the "O" so hard to type?

I huffed, looking at my phone. I needed some stress relief. I hit the contact button of a friend and called. "Hey, meet me at the Camel in thirty minutes."

#LadiesNite

"THAT ASSHOLE!!!" I huffed, slamming my third glass down on the bar. I was starting to feel the effects of my drinks, not that I'd admit that to anyone.

"You said that," Aimee sighed, sipping on her third glass of whiskey on the rocks, her yellow with rainbow trim wristband showing. I had forgotten that the Camel was hosting an LGBTQA event that night, and everyone got a band, according to your letter of sexuality. Mine was purple with rainbow trim since, sadly I was only an "ally." They had the letters painted on a rainbow flag so there was no confusion. L was red. G was orange. B was yellow. T was green. Q was blue. And A was purple. When we had walked in, I said we needed one red and one purple originally, which peeved Aimee as she went back to get herself a yellow one. "You know I'm bi, not a lesbian," she'd reminded me. I argued that she had told me before that she preferred girls to guys, but apparently that didn't mean anything. And that wasn't why we were here, anyway.

Aimee was one of my prettier friends. Long blond hair, which she stylistically shaved on one side. She had fair skin, thick rosy lips, and piercing blue eyes hiding behind long eyelashes. Just under the base of her skull on her neck was the word "Love" stylistically scrawled in curvy letters. Her long nails were always manicured in a pale purple, playing off the lilac tattoo on her inside forearm. Tonight she wore a denim jacket over a white lace cut-off tank top, showing off her toned abs against black ripped skinny-jeans.

"It's just ... I can't believe she paired me with that asshole," I stated angrily.

Aimee nodded knowingly, as she muttered, "You said that, too."

"Ok," I groused. She was annoying me a little right now. "Whose side are you on?"

Aimee gave me a pointed look, putting her drink down on the table. "Look, I know you hate the guy, but do you want to fail the class?"

I pouted. "No."

"Ok then," Aimee sighed, stirring the ice in her drink.

She gave a pained smile to a larger woman with buzzed hot pink hair and earlobe plugs. She wasn't unattractive, compared to some of the women I'd seen Aimee date. Most of them looked more like men who had boobs, while this woman looked more feminine with her pink hair. I had noticed the woman was trying to wave her down earlier for a drink. This was the second time.

"You should go to her," I stated, looking at the woman at the bar.

Aimee shook her head. "I'm not ditching my friend on her night of crisis," she said laughingly with a smile.

"Don't you mean 'bestie'?" I corrected, still smiling. Aimee looked away, still smiling as the band started their next song. It was Hudson and his band, Troubled Youths. He caught us staring and gave us a wink as his fingers plucked elegantly along the guitar strings. We'd be seeing each other later. A lot of each other later, I hoped. Recently he hadn't been as active in the bedroom. Stress, he said.

How could I describe Hudson? Well, he was everything Mike wasn't. Individual. A piece of art himself. His hair was dark and quaffed perfectly to the side, with messy locks draping a little over his ears, which were adorned with black plugs in the lobes. His full beard accentuated his angled nose and chiseled cheekbones.

His red plaid flannel shirt, which was usually buttoned to his neck, laid open showing off his chest and his detailed tattoo of two hands opening with the word "Dreamer" splayed between the fingertips. He had more, but that one was a personal favorite of mine. He was ruggedly handsome. And an artist, just like me. He sang and played acoustic guitar for his band that played regularly here, at The Camel. He had written a few of his own songs, but his voice when he sang "Wonderwall" would make any girl's legs turn to jelly. Just thinking about it made me tingly.

He was singing one of his originals now, "Your Taste." It was a slow romantic song. A panty-dropper, as his bandmates said. The way he moved with the song was sensual, intoxicating. It sent soothing chills down my spine.

I smiled back, drinking in the vision of him. "He's in rare form tonight," I stated. "Don't you think?" Aimee nodded, her eyes back to roving around the room. "Aimee?"

"What?" she asked, a little nervously, which didn't make much sense to me.

"Are you ok?"

She waved me off. "Yeah, fine." She reached for her drink again as she asked, "Hey, so how are things with you and Hudson?"

I rolled my eyes. Wasn't that the question of the year. "We're good I guess. I dunno." Aimee gave me a concerned pout at my answer. I could feel her psychically urging me on to spill. "Sometimes I feel like I'm not enough, or I'm holding him back." I didn't wait for Aimee to rebuke me before I scoffed. "I know. It's stupid." The song was dying down, with the drums beginning to amp up into their next song. It was a favorite of mine, which probably explained why Hudson was looking at us so intently.

Aimee grabbed my wrist and said, "Come on. We're dancing." I let her pull me to the center of the dance floor, our bodies close as we swayed to the music. I felt her hands on my hips, swaying me with her. I could see Hudson smiling back at us as I ran my hands over myself, catching my hair through my fingers. He enjoyed the show.

We danced until we were breathless, with the song dying out. Another bi woman on the other side of the stage flashed the band with a loud "WOOOO!!!" They had a groupie.

"Alright! We're going to take a fifteen-minute break!" Hudson called into the mic. He moved off the stage towards the back room.

"Man, I'm thirsty," I breathed out.

Aimee looked off to the side as she replied, "Hey, why don't you get us some drinks. I need to reapply my make-up."

I frowned, worry taking over me a little. "You need me to join?"

Aimee rolled her eyes. "I'll be fine. Go."

Whatever. I pulled out some cash for the bar as I made my way over. I leaned over the bar, showing my cash among the sea of arms also waving money for drinks.

"Hey," a voice behind me said. I turned to see an average sized guy wearing a V-neck t-shirt, that showed off a little chest hair. He had a curly red-headed mop for a hairstyle. He flashed a toothy grin behind thin lips. Clearly, he was a little drunk, but he thought I was drunker. I checked his wristband. Yellow. Bi. He might hit on me. If I decided to flirt back, though, my plans would be ruined with Hudson, replacing it with a ridiculous fight that left the sheets cold and empty.

"Hi," I replied nonchalantly, still looking for the bartender, the always personable, lovely, and stylish Jake.

"You having a good night?" I didn't dignify the no-name with an answer. "You want to make it better by coming over to my place?"

I pursed my lips before answering, "I'm sure there are plenty of guys here to take you up on that offer."

"I don't feel like playing bottom bitch tonight," he replied wistfully.

Oh ... my ... god ... EW! I believe my lunch was about to make an encore. I swallowed down my gag as I replied, "You know, on a list of shit I didn't need to know *ever*, that's probably at the top."

"Come on, what do you say?" He reached out for me, and I shied away. Seriously, NO THANK YOU.

"I say 'I have a boyfriend.'" Kind of.

"So?"

"I believe the lady said no." Thank God for Jake the bartender! Jake was fierce, and didn't take shit from anyone. And that modern Greyworm (or Jacob Anderson from Game of Thrones for the peons who don't watch. Google him.) look was really working for him tonight.

The no-name raised his hands in surrender and walked away. About time. Why don't the creeps ever get it the first time around? No means no. Just fucking NO.

I smiled at Jake, letting out a tired sigh. "My hero."

He waved me off, grabbing a rag to wipe up some spilt drink. "What's the drink?"

BZZZZZZZZZZZZZZZT

I hold up a finger, telling Jake to hold on for a second. My phone was needing me. Hey, maybe I got another follower on twitter. I checked my notifications, seeing my email.

Mike Davis: NaNoWriMo Mystery.

Nothing like a reminder that you're tied to your mortal enemy for a month to ruin a good night. Ok, minus the creep, a good night. Now I wouldn't be in the mood for Hudson later.

Clearly, my emotions showed. "Bad news?"

I pouted, putting my phone back into my pocket. "The worst." I let out a huff. Sorry Aimee. But I'm getting two drinks for myself. "What's the strongest thing you've got?" It was going to be one of those nights.

#TypewriterArt

I sat in my room, my hands poised on the typewriter. It had been two days since my Internet Writing's grade's fate had been tied to the mainstream Mike Davis's. As he promised, later that evening, he sent me an email with a plot-line, a schedule, and a link to where we were to post our chapters. Not only that, he posted the first chapter, introducing our story's hero, a Mr. Joe Black, *Private I.* Gag me. I appreciated his attempt at writing in film noir style for a mystery. But really? His writing didn't have the edge it needed. It read flat and dull, much like his personal style.

On the plus side, he did say in the email that I could have free reign on creating the female lead. Which is where I was at. Sitting at my typewriter, trying to figure out who our heroine lead would be.

My phone buzzed.

Where's the ch.? he texted.

Did I mention I was a little sprung for time?

Writing it now, I replied.

It wasn't like I was wasting my time and intentionally blowing this off. I was skipping our usual girls' night at The Camel. It was a sacred night for my friend Aimee and myself to get some free shots and catch up on the latest gossip. Even listen to Hudson play some music with his band. And if you say that I did all that two nights ago, I'll remind you that *that* isn't the point! The point is I was skipping it all tonight to write.

I was also thankful Ms. Harris gave us this day off, since she was at a conference that weekend to promote her several books of poetry. That meant I didn't have to see Mr. Cookie-cutter all day, which meant he wouldn't have been hounding me for my late chapter ... until now, that is.

My phone buzzed again.

How close r u 2 finishing?

I pursed my lips and looked at my typewriter. Usually, it made me feel creative and ideas would just pour out of my head and onto the page. But now, my typewriter's gift of creativity and ingenuity had abandoned me. I didn't want to say I had writer's block... but yeah, I was blocked.

Define finishing.

That was going to piss him off. But I didn't have time to deal with his inquisition.

My glasses! I always felt smarter with my glasses. Maybe that would be exactly what I needed to push back the block. I reached into my drawer and pulled out my black horn-rimmed lenseless glasses. My eyesight was perfect, so I didn't really need the glasses part. But they did make me look and feel smarter.

Now that I had given my brain all the supplies it needed to push the writer's block out, I should ...

BZZZZZZZZZZZZZZZZZZZZZZT

BZZZZZZZZZZZZZZZZZZZZZZZT

Ok, so now he's calling me. I picked up the phone. "Hello?"

"How much of the chapter do you have?"

I looked at the blank page. "Honestly?"

"Honestly."

"None."

He half hummed half groaned over the phone. "If you are trying to sabotage ..."

"No!" I quickly defended. "No sabotage. I'm just ..." I didn't want to say it. How could I say it? Admit to him that I'm blocked and can't figure out how to describe our heroine? Hell, admit that I don't even know who our heroine is? Admit to him that he's probably better at this than I am? I mean, that's what it meant, right? Words were supposed to be my lifeblood, and they were abandoning me right now.

"I'm blocked," I admitted in a small voice.

I expected him to reply with a snide comment. Or "Writer's block, what's that?" An ass like him would say something like that. I couldn't let him beat me at this. Writing was my game. He was just doing this as a hobby.

"Meet me at the library," he sighed over the phone, "in the café. Bring your laptop."

It took me by surprise. He wasn't going to poke fun at me for being blocked? "I don't write with a laptop."

"Well, bring whatever helps you write, then."

"Okay." Click.

I looked at my typewriter with a frown. Where was its case?

* ~ * ~ *

I sat in the café of the VCU library, which overlooked Shafer Court. It was a perfect perch to watch the campus nightlife pass by. The walkways were lit with street lamps, and students leaving their evening classes and walking out to their cars or dormitories. Maybe even trying to catch the last bus before they shut down for the night. The windows from floor to ceiling lit the room during the day, but at night, it was like sitting next to a void.

My typewriter was set up at a table, ready for when Mike decided to make his appearance.

"You have got to be kidding me."

I turned to see him with his satchel at his side as he stared wide-eyed at my typewriter.

"What?"

"What do you mean, 'What?' What the hell is that?" he asked, pointing at the typewriter.

I looked at it with a loving gaze. "It's a vintage Remington 5 typewriter. Black."

"Thank you," he said, making a very Chandler Bing-esque gesture with his hands, "but let me rephrase. What the hell is it *doing* here?"

"You said to bring what I write with. This is what I write with," I stated, gesturing to my typewriter.

He eyed me closely as he added, "Are you wearing lenseless glasses?"

I pushed the glasses up by the side and shrugged. "I feel smarter with glasses. But my vision's perfect, so..."

"No wonder you're blocked," he muttered, dropping his bag in the chair across from mine.

"Excuse me?" I hissed dangerously.

"You aren't taking your writing seriously," he clarified, crossing his arms, his gaze blank yet full of disappointment. I hated that look. "Hell, you don't take writing seriously, period."

I let out a bark of a laugh before laying into him. "I don't take writing seriously? You're saying *I* don't take writing seriously?!"

He nodded with a small smile, as if to say "Yes, that's exactly what I'm saying."

The growl that came out of my lips was purely guttural. "Who are *you* to judge me? You aren't even a writing major! You see, me, I'm an *artist*. This typewriter to me is the paintbrush that painted the Sistine Chapel. You - you just write for fun! You're a child with a crayon, while I work on masterpieces."

He rolled his eyes with a shrug as added, "Yet, I'm the one that's published."

I froze. Did my heart stop? Did I actually hear him correctly?

"It's funny, because Shakespeare got a lot of the same criticism you just gave me from his contemporaries," he muttered to himself with a little chuckle. "Look how that turned out for them."

"What?"

"Shakespeare—"

"Not that."

He sighed through his nose and looked away from the table, leaning back in his chair. "You don't have to major in something to be considered good at it." His green eyes settled on me as he added the final blow, "Of the two of us here, one is a writing student and the other is a published short-story author. So, maybe you could learn a thing or two from me, like, I don't know, not getting caught up in looking the part of the writer to forget to actually write ... or humility. Take your pick."

I sat back down in my chair and remained silent. I could hear his fingertips tapping on the table impatiently as I processed what he said. "You're a published author?" It was a question, but I more stated it than asked.

"Yeah. Have been for two years now. It's actually why I chose creative writing as my *minor*," he explained a little haughtily, running a hand through his light brown hair.

I frowned, looking at my typewriter. How could that be? I tried so hard to be considered an artist, a writer to be taken seriously. And this guy, this asshole who wrote the blandest material, was published. He almost never had description in his writing. I remember one assignment we had, he just wrote dialogue with the only identifiers for his characters was their shirt colors.

"I know," he said, rolling his eyes, as if he could read my mind. "'But you only give minimal details,'" he mocked, throwing up air quotes. Who did that anymore? It was such a 1999 gesture. "I write like I think. Direct and to the point. I don't like when writing gets mired in the details."

I gave him a pointed glare. "You're talking about my writing now, aren't you?"

He gave me a pearly white sarcastic smile as he leaned in and replied, "You aren't the only writer who does it." He licked his lips as he shot a glance at my typewriter, then back at me. "Look, a typewriter might be a great writing tool, but it's not the only one. And since we have to post chapters daily in a timely manner and online, for expedience sake, can we lose it and opt for a computer?"

I pouted. "But it's really nice typing in the park..."

"Please." His eyes held an urgency that made me pause.

Maybe a typewriter wasn't the best tool for me at the moment. After all, Michelangelo didn't paint David.

We sat at a computer, blankly staring at a screen as we brainstormed, our heads in our hands as we took in the blank word document on the monitor. "I think ... my brain is fried," I grumbled.

"Mine, too," Mike replied. He blew out his cheeks, making that bored horse sound with his lips. "Where's the plotline?"

I reached in my purse and pulled out a folded piece of paper and handed it to him with one hand, while the other still held my head up. This was starting to get ridiculous, but a part of me knew that once we got the ball rolling on our book, and the gears started turning, we'd be golden. Which is probably what Ms. Harris had also felt deep in her gut. That or this was just a bluff, and as long as an attempt was made, everyone would get an A. But I doubted my second hypothesis.

Mike grabbed it and unfolded it, reading over his writing. He leaned back in his chair, breathing deeply.

"Alright, this chapter we are introducing the female lead to the hero, from her perspective."

"Which would be great if we could figure out a believable heroine. Why is she there? What's her purpose?" I posed. Because, honestly, that's where I got stuck.

"That was your job," Mike said, tapping his index finger on the desk.

I frowned at him. "That's where I got blocked. Your plotline left no suitable room for a heroine," I replied, pointing out. "Look at the plot, the only thing she's useful for is a sexual distraction for Mr. Joe Black."

Mike scowled, looking away from me and muttering, "We wouldn't have had this issue if you had helped come up with a plot."

"Fine!" I snapped, ripping the plot away from Mike's hands. I began ripping up the paper as Mike's green eyes went wide.

"What the HELL are you DOING!?!?!" he almost screeched at me.

I threw the pieces in the trash bin, ignoring Mike's protests. The only thing we could do was move forward. That plot was what was holding us back. "We're starting from scratch."

"Oh my God," he groaned, his head in his hands as his eyes frantically followed his paper into the trashcan. I could tell he thought we were screwed. But we weren't. I had a plan. Plus, keeping him in suspense like this was actually a little entertaining. After the critique he put me through last semester, he deserved it... maybe only a little, but still! It was priceless watching him frantically pull at his hair as the words "We're doomed!" whirled through his mind. They were practically visible with the ghostly fear in his eyes.

"I think we should re-write a popular story," I stated, putting my hands together and facing him.

He seemed to calm a little, but when his gaze shifted to me with a huff, I could tell he wanted more than just a suggestion. He wanted a plan since I just ripped up the one he had worked on yesterday. His voice was almost a croak as he asked, "Re-write a popular story." I nodded. He straightened up, and I could tell he was trying to keep calm, but inside he was panicking. Like a duck on water, as my Mom would say. "Like what story?"

"Like a famous love story," I answered excitedly. "That way we already have the plot points, we can just make it modern."

Mike pursed his lips. "What famous love story were you thinking about?"

Suddenly I felt self-conscious. "R-Romeo and Juliet." The story had crossed my mind several times as we'd gone over and over the plot. Something about "Star-crossed lovers" rang in my head from our previous conversation. It seemed like a good place to start. And I'd get my dystopian romance if things went the way I planned. See? I'm more than my looks up here.

Mike sat up, his gaze off in the distance with a serious squint. "I hate Romeo and Juliet."

My eyes went wide. What planet was this asshole from? "You hate ...?"

"I'll do it," he interrupted me, taking me by surprise, "on one condition." I nodded for him to continue. "Everything's reversed and it's a comedy."

"Uh... a comedy?"

"Yeah."

I let that sink in. Romeo and Juliet as a comedy. It didn't make sense. They both died in the end. Suicide over heartbreak. How could that be funny? And don't complain about spoilers! You've had 422 years to read it. Catch up! "How will we make it a comedy?" I asked cagily. This wasn't the way I had planned this conversation going, but I'd play along for a little while.

Mike shrugged nonchalantly. "Montagues and Capulets are good friends who arrange a marriage between their two kids, Romeo and Juliet, who actually hate each other."

I frowned as I tried to piece that with the rest of the story. I was fairly certain it wouldn't work. How would they die for each other? *And still make it funny?* "What about the rest of the plot points. How would they figure in?"

Mike paused to think, and I smiled. I had him. It was impossible. He'd realize that, and I'd get my futuristic dystopian romance.

I scowled when he snapped his fingers in his "Aha" moment. "They still meet at the party. Romeo decides he hates her, but at the party, it's announced they are to be married. The balcony scene turns out pretty much the same with Juliet asking why does he have to be Romeo, but more in a 'Why do I have to marry him?' sense. Romeo talks to the priest to figure a way out of it. They still get married. Juliet hired Tybalt to murder Romeo right after the wedding. Romeo killed him instead." He stopped trying to think his way around Romeo's exile.

I smiled. He was stuck. I opened my mouth to speak, but he held up a finger with an intelligent smirk. A smirk that told me he had somehow figured it out. Again.

"Tybalt was actually a wanted assassin for hire, which is why Juliet went to him. So, Romeo is awarded lands by the prince for his contribution to society. Juliet goes to an alchemist for a way to get her out of the marriage, which is when she's presented with the fake poison. After the funeral, Romeo goes to the tomb to make sure she's dead with a poison of his own disguised as a flask of water. She wakes up, stabs him. And after almost a day of being 'dead,'" he did the air quotes again. Really? Whatever, "she'd obviously be thirsty. So she pilfers his flask and drinks it, and dies when she realizes she poisoned herself." He smiled as if he were proud of himself.

All I could do was stare. How? How could he just jovially crap on a classic? Not only a classic, but the most romantic classic in all of literature. How was there not some god or goddess of love behind him beating him to death with a Shakespeare anthology? Did karma mean nothing in the real world? What about poetic justice?

He let out a victorious chuckle. "You can thank me when you're ready," he said, turning to the computer, pulling up the school website and going to his email. "I'll just email Professor Harris about the change in our plans."

My mouth hung open as he continued to type the email to our professor. He snuck a glance at me, and with a scoff he asked, "Cat got your tongue?"

"I-I just don't get you," I finally stated. Suddenly he looked innocent, as if he had no idea what could cause that reaction from me. "Are you heartless? Do you have no soul? Do you just enjoy bringing others and their works down?"

Now he looked confused. "What are you talking about?"

"How do you *not* like Romeo and Juliet?!" I almost screeched. Maybe I was overreacting. But honestly. HOW?

He laughed. "It's a story about two kids who commit suicide after a rushed marriage that only lasted four days."

I gasped. What lies? "It was more than four days!"

"Read it again," he laughed as he turned back to type.

"And they were not kids!"

"Juliet was thirteen, and Romeo was seventeen."

"And they were in love!"

"Bull," Mike scoffed. My eyes went wide as he denied the most poignant fact of the whole play. "Romeo was head over heels for Rosalind an hour before he met Juliet." My voice refused to work as my mouth hung open in shock. It had to be shock. I was fairly certain I was showing symptoms, maybe. Dammit, I'm a writer, not a doctor!

"I'll get the first chapter written up tonight, since it starts with Romeo anyway." Mike finished up his email, hitting send enthusiastically with a smile.

I rose an eyebrow at his victorious behavior as he packed up his stuff and logged off the computer. This wasn't the story we were supposed to be writing ... How did my plan get so twisted? "What, am I supposed to be writing from Juliet's perspective?"

He looked at me blankly. "Yeah. That's what you wanted, right?" When my unamused frown didn't alleviate, he sighed. "I find it hard to believe that you can't write a character who hates another character."

I flashed him a rueful smile as I replied. "No, it's not hard. All I've got to do is think about you."

Mike grinned back at me. "That's the spirit! I'll see you later!" With that, he took off from the library, leaving me fuming over our novel. He wanted a hateful Juliet? Fine. I'd give him a hateful Juliet.

#2canPlaythatGame

I sat in Hudson's room, leaning on his shoulder cozily, scrolling through my phone the next day. It was my turn to post, and I was checking my Facebook while I waited for Mike to post the new chapter. Oddly enough, Mike seemed to be taking his dear sweet time, but I wasn't going to complain about it. Hudson lay relaxed next to me, reading his favorite book, *The Great Gatsby*.

Technically, Hudson and I were roommates, because it was cheaper to get a two-bedroom apartment than a one. That and we'd been something of an item for a little over a year. We'd never really talked about an official relationship. Neither of us really like labels, and why complicate things with a definitive name. We agreed on most things socially, politically, and artistically. He was like me, and we felt safe together to be ourselves.

Ding!

I blinked myself out of my stupor, a little peeved to see a text from Mike. Also a little annoyed that I took my phone off silence while Hudson and I were snuggled up together. I opened my txt app and read, "1 st ch. up," with a link attached below. I opened the link on my phone, bracing myself for the droll intro of our hero, Romeo. As soon as the site loaded, my eye was drawn to the banner. Apparently, he'd been playing with photoshop for most of the day. There was a cartoony drawing of a heart being stabbed with an ornate dagger, and scrolled underneath it read, *"For never was there a tale of more Regret than this of Romeo and his Juliet."* Punny. I rolled my eyes as I moved on to the chapter itself.

The scene opened with Romeo complaining to a friend about his doomed love of Rosalind, because he'd just heard news of his pending betrothal. His friend tried to brighten his spirits by saying things like, *"She's probably not that bad,"* *"I bet she'll be pretty,"* and *"It's not the end of the world."* (Sadly, I'll admit I laughed a little at his friend. But that's only because I knew how this was going to end.)

It moved onto the party where it was announced that Romeo's betrothed was to be Juliet, and the small smile that had somehow found its way to my face (don't ask me how. I *wasn't* enjoying the chapter) fell. She was me. And I don't mean in the vague descriptions way where she *could* be me. I mean if I decided to dress in Renn. Faire garb, I would be this Juliet. Petit frame with a decently sized bust (not that I'm bragging). Check. Adorned in what I would call a boho chic style, if it existed at the time. You know. Flowers braided into the almost black (excuse me. I picked this dye myself, and it is JET Black, thank you) hair, simple rings on each finger with a simple necklace, and a simple yet beautiful dress. Check. Dark, penetrating (yet chocolatey, which he missed in the description) eyes under thick dark eyebrows. Check. A soft, yet angular face with prominent cheekbones, set off by thick wine-red lips (my effing signature!). Check. I was seething. For an asshole who hates description, he seemed to describe me in every detail, except in this annoying fashion that also highlighted my flaws ... and for some reason gave me – sorry, *Juliet* a bad case of "resting bitch-face," as they called it.

Hudson seemed to sense my fury. Maybe because I was no longer leaning on his shoulder but glaring down at my phone. "Are you ok?" he asked, turning a page in his book.

"Yeah," I growled, scrolling back through the chapter to skim through the details. Oh, I was going to get that vanilla bastard back if he wanted to play that way. I know. Most would say forgive and forget. But when a line was crossed, you know being petty was a lot more fun sometimes. Especially when you weren't afraid of the bridges you'd burn. And, boy, did he cross that line.

I smiled as I saw that he'd left Romeo's description rather lackluster (much like the writer himself). Vague descriptions of unkempt hair and kind of boy-next-door vibes. Possibly even relatable. Yeah. That was going to change. I was going to immortalize every flaw of Mike's, just as he'd done me.

I sprung up off the bed, grabbing my suede fringed purse and notebook, though I doubted I'd need it. "Hudson, where are the keys?" I asked, fishing my glasses out of the desk. Being my roommate ... lover? ... whatever, he frequently borrowed my white 1998 Chevrolet Geo Prizm. I know, it's old, but the sucker still runs. It was a proud moment for myself when I bought it two years ago for a couple hundred bucks. It had a few quirks, being an old car, but it still got me around town.

He frowned at my sporadic behavior, but I ignored it, feeling the inspiring fuel of payback running through my mind. "Why? Where're you going?" He was sitting up now, moving off the bed.

"Library," I answered quickly. "I've got this project I'm working on, and I need to type it up." I stopped when I saw him pouting. "What?"

He reached out to me, snagging a finger in one of my ripped jean's belt loops, pulling me closer to him. I rolled my eyes at his flirty gesture as I let him pull me in. "I was just hoping you'd stick around for a little dinner and fun," he said, his icy blue eyes roving over me.

I rolled my eyes. He was only doing this because I said I was leaving. Usually, he would sit quietly without even an inkling of wanting sex even all the way up to when we'd go to sleep. It was infuriating sometimes, but I'd somehow gotten used to its simplicity.

I gave him a short peck on the lips before removing his fingers from my belt loops. Normally, I'd say yes. But now I was motivated to put some asshole in his place. And getting down would ruin that motivation. "I won't be long," I reassured, patting his cheek playfully. I moved away, turning from his disappointed frown, as I asked again, "Now, where are the keys?"

"Bowl, kitchen counter," Hudson huffed behind me, the bed squeaking as he flopped back on it.

I nodded, stepping out of the room towards the kitchen at the front, but I stopped in the doorway.

Something about Mike's description gnawed at me a little, and I turned, a little self-conscious as I asked, "I don't have resting bitch face ... do I?"

Hudson eyed me with confusion, pursing his lips together as he tried to form an answer. After a pregnant pause, he asked, "Is this supposed to be a trick question?"

My mind went blank as my face fell to a scowl. I quickly snatched a rolled-up sock pair sitting on his dresser next to me and pegged it at him as hard as I could before turning on my heel and stomping out. "Fucking jerk!"

I heard him jump off the bed and run to follow me, calling after me, "Rebel, come on! You can't just ask me a loaded question like that and not expect me to be honest!"

"Oh, go fuck yourself!" I howled back, not turning to look at him as I snatched up the keys for the car and headed to the front door. I felt the tears sting my eyes, but held fast to my fury. I'm not going to cry. I'm not going to cry.

As I turned the knob on the front door, I heard him yell back at me, "Well, fuck you too!" before stomping back into his room. Without a second thought,

I left. I didn't need his prima-donna attitude right now. Yes, Hudson did have a flair for the dramatic. Sometimes it was sweet. Others, it made me want to smash his face through one of his many mirrors.

And this was Mike's fault anyway! If he hadn't made me self-conscious about how I looked, I wouldn't have asked Hudson in the first place. It all just fueled my inner anger at my project-mate.

As I slammed the front door of our apartment behind me, I felt the tear trail down my cheek, which I wiped away quickly, pushing down that lump in my throat. I made my way to the car, slamming the door as I sat in the driver's seat. The squeal the tires made as I high-tailed it out of the parking lot echoed off the apartment buildings.

I squeezed the steering wheel tight and chewed on my lower lip, using those feelings to drive my anger through my upset mind. This wasn't the time to cry about what people thought of me. Usually, I don't even care. But for some reason I did this time. And I refused to let it get to me. I had to use this to get even.

I slammed into a parking spot and made my way into the library, finding an open computer in a quiet spot and getting to work on the balcony scene. Surprisingly, I didn't even need my glasses for the imagination boost. The words seemed to fly from my mind onto the page. My fingers clacked against the keys harshly as I muttered along with my writing, *"Romeo, Romeo. Why the Hell did they pick Romeo!?"*

#Back2Class

Next class was interesting to say the least. When I had finished the last chapter, I was actually pretty proud of it. It was funny, scathing, and honestly kind of cathartic. As I posted the chapter, I realized couldn't wait to come into class today and see Mike's wounded pride at my derisive description of his Romeo.

Of course, Hudson and I patched up our disagreement as soon as I got home with a nice glass of wine and a make-out session. I offered make-up sex, but it was too late when I got back, and all Hudson wanted to do was sleep.

Not that Hudson and I needed to make-up. It was Mike's fault anyway. He was the one I was truly upset with, not Hudson. I told him that and apologized, which he agreed was only logical. I couldn't be mad at him for something someone else wrote. That and Hudson insisted on walking me to class this morning, which was uncharacteristically sweet.

As we walked up to the classroom, I noted a sign that said "Sit with your NaNoWriMo Group." I was then met with Mike beaming at me from his computer. Not really the reaction I was looking for. "Is that him?" Hudson asked, a little growl in his voice.

I squeezed his hand and smiled. "Don't worry about him."

"You shouldn't let anyone make you feel that shitty," he added, glaring at Mike almost territorially. Honestly, it was a little unnerving. Hudson wasn't usually the jealous type. Well, actually, I never really gave him a reason to be in the first place.

"Chill" I laughed, letting go of him. "I already took care of Mike." Hudson gave me a skeptical look, causing me to frown. He knew I could fight my own battles. I was never some damsel in distress. "Thank you for walking me to class," I added, standing on tippy toes to kiss Hudson's cheek. Did I mention he was tall? And his beard smelled of evergreen (must have been using that beard oil I bought him for his birthday a few weeks ago).

Hudson pulled away adding sweetly, "You tell me if he keeps up that shit. I'll come down here and set him right."

I chuckled at his sudden protective attitude. It was a little charming. "I'll set him right first. Don't worry. Now go." I shooed him off, a small smile finding its way to my face as Hudson left the building.

I turned back to Mike, who was still smiling pearly white, but he seemed to be eyeing me more curiously. My own smile fell away as I scowled at him. Shouldn't he be a little more upset? I did just publicly roast his ass to our class, just as he did me the other day. I made my way over to him, plopping down into the chair next to him as I asked, "What?"

Mike shook his head smugly as he replied, "I didn't think Lumberjack was your type."

I rolled my eyes. "*Individual* is my type." He made a mock "Ah," face as I replied. "And two, Hudson isn't a lumberjack. He's a musician. Guitarist."

Mike smirked, that impish glint in his green eyes came back as he said, "Lemme guess. He fronts an Oasis cover band that frequents the park." There was sarcasm in his tone, but I wasn't sure why.

I blinked at Mike confused. "Who?"

"Oasis," he repeated. "You know, 'Champagne Supernova' and 'Wonderwall'?" I froze as his words ran through my mind. This humdrum asshole knew that song? Knew those songs?! Hudson always sang those. As he looked over my shocked face, his smile grew larger with his vibrant green eyes filling with shock and delight. "Oh my God," he almost screeched through his laughter. His eyes glistened with gleeful tears. "I was kidding," he sputtered through his laughter as he wiped a tear from his eyes.

I scowled at him losing himself at my lover's expense. "You know he's actually quite good," I attempted to defend. Mike nodded with false assurance as he did his best to suppress his chuckles. "He performs fairly regularly at The Camel and some of the other bars."

Still laughing, Mike shook his head with disbelief, his hair falling a little out of place as he leaned forward, pinching the bridge of his nose. "You can't be serious." When I nodded my answer, his guffawing started anew. I scowled at him taking his time to calm down. "Well," he coughed, sobering from his laughing fit, and turning to the computer, "Good for him."

I could tell he was being facetious, but I wasn't going to give him the satisfaction of being hurt by his judgements. I was still a little curious why he wasn't hurt by mine. "So, what did you think of Romeo's description?" I asked, pointedly.

Mike shot me a knowing look. Maybe my topical segue wasn't so subtle. Whatever. His pinkish lips were graced with a small smile as he said, "Actually, I found it very apt for Juliet's character to only focus on the negative. It added some depth."

I quirked an eyebrow at his opinion. "*Only* Juliet's character focused on the negative?" Mike nodded, not looking at me as he checked his email. Excuse me! After reading his chapter, I was ... I mean *Juliet* was in the right to describe Romeo as such an ugly, plain asshole who only cared about himself and his status. I grit my teeth as I added, "Didn't Romeo describe Juliet as having, 'resting bitch-face'?"

"Yeah, and?" Mike replied nonchalantly.

"You wouldn't call that negative?"

Mike shrugged. "Not necessarily. It depends on how you look at it." I narrowed my eyes, urging him to explain. "Most strong female characters can be described with 'resting bitch face.' It doesn't mean they're unattractive. I mean, if you googled 'resting bitch-face,' do you know who shows up?" I didn't need to answer for him to continue. "Nine times out of ten, it's Scarlett

O'Hara, who I'd say is far from unattractive. It just means Juliet has a permanently relaxed scowl on her face."

"Then just say I've got a permanent scowl! And don't call me a bitch!" I snapped at him.

Mike raised an eyebrow at my outburst, and now a concerned gleam in his eyes that I never would have dreamed of seeing. "I never called you a ... I never meant to call *you* a ..." he stammered. "You *aren't* Juliet."

"Oh, please," I derided. I wasn't in the mood for excuses. "You described her exactly like me."

A faint blush crossed his face before he cleared his throat. He seemed flustered. "No I didn't."

"Yeah. The bohemian dressed brunette with brown eyes, prominent cheekbones, and my signature red lips," I argued. Any idiot who knew us could figure out it was me he was describing.

Mike shrugged. "That could've been anybody," he muttered, distractedly scrolling down a page on his computer.

I rolled my eyes. Anybody. Yeah, right. I knew it was me. I couldn't really put my finger on exactly why he was suddenly acting all sheepish. If you're going to insult me, at least have the balls to own up to it. But, I was wasting mind power and time trying to figure him out.

"Whatever," I grumbled, rolling my eyes. Professor Harris had entered the computer lab with a swish of her black and white chevron poncho, and pulled up what looked like a schedule.

"Welcome back, class. I hope everyone used the time off well. Got some good headway on their novels," Ms. Harris begun, looking over our class with beaming smiles. "Because, I don't know if any of you noticed," she continued, pointing to the schedule, "but we have a week and a half before Thanksgiving break. And the novels are due as soon as we get back. So there's no time to dawdle around." She lifted up a stack of papers, dropping them next to one student on the far end of the lab. "Take one and pass it down," she instructed to the student, who obliged.

"This is the schedule in which each group will present their NaNoWriMo project. If you have a scheduling conflict, see me after class. Now, get to work."

There was silence between Mike and I as we waited for our schedules to come around. I wasn't going to say anything to him until he apologized. And since he was a grade A asshole, that would likely happen when Hell experienced its first blizzard.

"I'm sorry," he said sincerely, handing me the stack of schedules as they were passed down. I was shocked. Absolutely shocked. "Really," he added, eyeing me apologetically. "I'm sorry. It was an asshole move on my part. I didn't realize I'd ..." he cut himself off, with a frown. His eyes gained an odd sorrowful look before he shook his head. "It doesn't matter. I'll go in and change it immediately."

I think I felt my jaw drop at his apology. Where was this apology last year when he said my writing earned a failing grade?! Despite myself, I said a small, "Thank you."

I might be going crazy.

#friends

"So, I'm not sure if I'm getting this right," Aimee said, tapping a finger against her glass. We were eating at one of the on-campus restaurants. They had the best pizza. I was a sucker for a well-made white pizza. "Asshole Mike, who you were bashing all last week, is now an OK guy?"

I nodded. It wasn't a hard concept, so I'm not sure why she was having such difficulty understanding it.

"When did *that* happen?"

I shrugged. "I dunno. He just doesn't seem so bad recently. Nice, even." It was true. He and I really seemed to be clicking recently. The past week went by oddly without a hitch between Mike and me. It was odd having more spats between Hudson and I than my writing rival.

Something changed in Mike's behavior since the "bitch-face" incident, as I was calling it. True to his word, he took the descriptor down during that class period. And since then, we resolved to meet up at the library every day, and edit each other's chapters, since it was something we'd have to work on together anyway.

Interestingly enough, those meetings were quickly turning into the highlight of my days. One of us would buy the coffee. Then we'd go find a comfortable spot in the library to discuss the chapter, going over jokes and jabs at each other's expense. For the book, you know? After the first meeting, I started to realize how funny he actually was. He may be blunt in his observations, but his razor witty sarcasm was always sharp and ready. Then we'd post the chapter together before we went back to our regular lives. It was ... nice. ... Relaxing, even.

Hudson and I on the other hand ... Well, let's *not* get into that, shall we?

"Then I'm sorry, I just don't get it. You've been bitching about this guy for a year."

I scowled at her. "I haven't been bitching."

"Last semester, you said, I quote, 'Talentless hack. Who's he to say that I can't write for shit?'"

I looked away. "That was last year."

There was dead silence over the table for a minute before she asked the question, "Does it have to do with you and Hudson?" Where the hell did that come from!?

I frowned at her. "What!? No!"

She held her hands up defensively, "It's ok. I know you two have been fighting a little more, recently."

"Who told you that?" I growled. I was fairly sure I knew the answer, but I was certain I wasn't going to like it. If it was who I thought it was, he had no reason to be talking about us *to anyone* behind my back. Not to mention he was the one starting things to begin with!

She shrugged nonchalantly, "Hudson."

I set my jaw. "Did he, now?" Nope, didn't like that answer. We were going to fight as soon as I got home. I could feel it. Maybe I'd start this one. "Did he tell you what we've been arguing about? It's that I've been assigned to a project with Mike. He thinks that means cheating, when let's be honest, he's the only one that's cheated before."

Aimee frowned, saying, "That was a long time ago, though."

"Five months is not long," I argued, "And why does that mean I'm automatically cheating for working on an assignment!?"

She opened her mouth to defend him but was interrupted by the ding of the front door, which I faced, seeing Mike walk into the establishment. Wow, did he have impeccable timing. He waved with a smile, his teeth white and perfect. I dropped my angry demeanor for a more favorable smile and waved back to him. Aimee followed my gaze, turning to Mike, taking in his white button-down shirt under a long sleeved blue sweater and belted worn jeans. His sleeves were rolled up, and he carried a notebook under a lightly tanned arm.

Aimee turned back to me, eyeing my smile before humming, "Uh-huh."

I glowered back at her. "What?"

"Nothing," Aimee said defensively. It wasn't believable. She knew I didn't believe it was just nothing. She shook her head as she said, "I get it, if his looks are anything to go by."

I rolled my eyes. "Looks aren't everything, you know."

Aimee frowned somberly as she muttered, "Yeah, but it can really help brushing over their faults."

I frowned, getting the feeling that maybe I had missed something going on with my closest friend. "Are you ok?" I asked, genuinely concerned. I may be self-involved sometimes, but I wasn't uncaring. Especially when it looked like I had a friend in need.

"Fine," she replied with a smile. It wasn't a sincere smile, but I let it go.

#LuvLuvLuv

"I can't believe you forgave him!"

"Look, Professor Harris said our partners were non-negotiable. I *have* to work with him," I defended as I packed up my to-be-edited chapter and a notebook and pen. "It's easier for both of us if we let the stupid shit slide. Plus, he took it down." I really didn't have time for this argument, *again.* I was already running late for my meeting with Mike. We were going over our schedules for the break, which started tomorrow. And the faster I got to that meeting, the faster I could get back and pack for my trip home tomorrow. I patted my pants looking around my room, muttering, "Where is my phone?"

Hudson ignored me. "'Stupid shit?' He called you a bitch. You're just ok with that?"

I sighed. This was the fifth time we've had this argument this week. It was tiring. "One. He didn't mean me directly. Two. He took it down as soon as I expressed a problem with it. And Three. He apologized, which is more than what you did!"

"Oh, now I'm the asshole?!"

"Kinda!" I snapped, slinging my bag on my shoulder. He stood in my doorway, arms crossed. My scowl matched his own as I growled. "Move."

"Do you like him?"

Where the Hell did that come from? It took me completely by surprise. "What!?" I balked, half laughing.

He shifted forward an inch as he asked, "Are you attracted to him?" His amber eyes boring into mine. Usually, they were sultry, but recently they burned with an intense frustration I didn't get.

I stepped back, looking at him confused. "What the Hell does that have to do with anything?"

"It's the only reason I can think of given your recent behavior," he replied with a small sneer.

I squinted at him, my mind flooding with confusion. I took a step back at his words. *My behavior?* "Who are you, my mother?"

"You still haven't answered my question," he stated, ignoring my comment again.

"Because it's a stupid question!" I snapped back.

"Is it?! Because you still haven't answered it!" he howled at me. His hands were balled into fists as his arms shook in anger. But I knew Hudson would never hurt me. "You two could be going on dates behind my back. Or fucking. I don't know."

I scowled at him. "I've *never* cheated on you. Which is more than I can say for you."

"Is that why you're with him? To even the score?"

"WHAT SCORE!?" I screeched.

Suddenly it clicked. "Is that what this is?" I scoffed. "You're *jealous*?" That was rich. I mean, I should have noticed sooner. The increase in arguments, the constant need to know where I was going. Of course he was jealous. But it was his idea to not label us as officially going out anyway. If I remember correctly, he said he didn't want to "complicate things." And on top of that, he was the only one out of the two of us who'd cheated before.

I laughed at how ludicrous it was.

His arms dropped to his sides, his amber eyes losing that fiery glare. "I'm not jealous," he said, tiredly. "I just wish you'd stay here. ... With me."

"And do what?" I scoffed. "You haven't touched me more than a peck on the lips in over a month!"

"I'll take you right now if you stay," he replied quickly. He meant for it to be kind of sexy, but the frustration in his eyes and slight anger in his tone made it decidedly not. He didn't want me romantically. He wanted me to prove a point. Sorry. I don't work that way.

"Tempting as that sounds," I replied, my voice dripping with sarcasm. "You know I can't. I've got a project due as soon as we get back from break."

He nodded dejectedly, his half-hearted smile more a frown. "Right," he muttered, stepping back into the hallway. "I'm being ridiculous." A part of me was apprehensive of the way he said it. But the other part, the overwhelming majority of my being was just happy to be done with the argument. I was already so late.

I made my way out of the apartment, snagging the keys out of the bowl and down to my car. The sky started to roll with dark clouds. The weather did indicate a storm was headed this way tonight. I quickly cranked up the car and sped out of the complex.

It wasn't until I was halfway there that I realized I left my phone thanks to our distracting argument. But it was too late to turn back. And I knew where Mike would be waiting for me anyway. It just left me feeling unsettled, not having any communicative device in case of emergency. It felt like I was missing something crucial ... like a limb. Oh well. Social media would just have to wait until I returned home.

#BooksNCoffee

I waltzed into the library coffee shop, and see Mike sitting there waiting for me, two coffees at the ready, and I immediately felt a sense of relief flood through me. It was odd that meeting up for classwork was more relaxing than going home and having another argument with Hudson. I mean the logic didn't exactly follow, but that didn't change the fact it was true.

Mike stood as soon as his gaze landed on mine, almost as if he sensed my presence. He grabbed both coffees and made his way over to me, and I smiled. As he closed the gap between us, he offered one coffee to me, which I took eagerly. I took a sip, needing the caffeine to calm my nerves. The warm, sweet liquid hit my tongue, and I immediately felt at ease. Mike always got my coffee just right. I let out a small contented hum and he gave me a weird look but shrugged it off.

"Ok," I sighed as the effects of the coffee rushed through me. I reached into my bag, grabbing my folder before handing it to him, saying, "Chapter seventeen."

He took it happily, walking back to the table where he'd left his bag.

After the last fifteen meetings, I'd learned things about his preferences, like his preference to proof or edit a solid copy with a red pen than just reading it through on the computer. It made the flash drive I'd begun holding the chapters on mandatory for each meeting.

He flipped open my basic blue folder that held the new chapter, settling in to read it. I sipped on my coffee as I watched his verdant eyes rove over the lines I'd written as he tapped his red pen against the table. A tick that I'd learned to live with. The first time I sat there watching him read, tapping that infernal red pen, it nearly drove me up a wall. He paused to make a change, then kept reading as if nothing happened. I leaned over to try and see the change he made, but he turned the page too quickly. Focused on that chapter. I guess that's a good sign. He made a small chuckle at a joke I'd written, and I grinned even though he couldn't see. That was definitely a good sign. I treated myself to a victorious sip as he continued.

I'll say this about Mike, he reads a lot faster than I do. He made a couple more marks and notes, then continued reading, nodding along as he finished up the chapter.

"Ok," he breathed, shutting the folder gently, passing it back to me. "It's really good. I liked the meeting between Juliet and Tybalt."

"You did?" I asked, a little surprised. I'd hoped he would have liked it, but it was so difficult to write it out, I was worried it had come off strained.

"Yeah," he said with an emphatic nod. "You got Tybalt just right. He didn't seem overzealous with the idea of killing Romeo, but it was also clear that what Juliet was hiring him to do wasn't new to him." I grinned a little, feeling good that I got that right. Again, writing that scene felt like pulling teeth, but if it turned out good, who was I to complain.

He licked his lips nervously as he continued on, "The only thing I think Professor Harris might have with the chapter ..."

I smirked at his skirting around the subject. Recently, whenever he wanted to make a big change that he knew I'd argue with, he used Professor Harris as a cover. But I wasn't born yesterday. "You mean you have with the chapter," I corrected, taking another sip of my coffee.

He chewed on his pink lip, and I chewed on mine a little, wondering if it was as soft as it looked. ... Wait ... WHAT?! No. I didn't mean. ... Whatever. I'm with Hudson.

"Yeah, just I was thinking we could leave out the wedding night, but you wrote it out ... in detail," he said nervously, and was he ... blushing?

I decided to ignore it. I'm with Hudson.

I leaned back in my chair, crossing my arms as I replied, "I felt it provided great context for Juliet hiring an assassin like Tybalt."

"Okay," he replied, "and I agree with that completely. But writing it out makes it seem like Romeo's raping her."

I frowned. "He is raping her."

He pursed his lips, not looking at me but the table. There was silence between us as I tried to decipher his expression. It was a kind of pensive yet confused look. "Ok, but that makes it seem like Romeo wants that, when he isn't exactly consenting either." How does that make sense? Sometimes Mike's logic wasn't entirely on par with mine, but even by basic standards, how was Romeo's feelings even relevant? My look clearly told him what I was thinking. "Look, I'd get it if he was evil and sought to dominate her, but that clearly isn't Romeo from the previous chapters. He's only consummating the marriage because it's what's expected of him."

I scoffed at his defense, "That doesn't make it right. Rape is rape."

"No, you're right, it doesn't," he agreed. "But we've based this back during the early renaissance, which is when arranged marriages and these kinds of wedding nights happened." He paused as he seemed to try and find his words.

I leaned in with a sigh. "You said they consummate the marriage." He nodded, knowing that's what he'd written in the chapter plans. "You said that was why she hires Tybalt to kill him." Again he nodded. "I don't see why there's an issue with the scene then."

"Ok, but this leaves out any reconciliation or redemption for Romeo," Mike stated. "He's not supposed to be the bad guy."

"He is for Juliet," I argued. Mike frowned as I continued, "And reconciliation? This ends with them trying to kill each other."

He chewed the inside of his cheek as he mumbled, "I thought maybe we could change that." I looked at him confused, but he shook that off as he offered, "Look, just the way you have it written is uncharacteristic for Romeo."

I scowled at him now. "You want me to alter Juliet's feelings on her own rape in order for the audience to like Romeo more?" the question had a dangerous tone to it.

"No," Mike replied, surprising me a little by his previous stance. I crossed my arms again, letting him continue. "I think she should be enraged, and you wrote that very well. But I was thinking their wedding night would have been more of a bedding ceremony, which was accurate for that time, and pushes them both to perform. That puts Romeo in the same boat as Juliet. And that redirects her rage to anyone who set up the marriage, and a little at Romeo for following through with it. But the audience can still sympathize with both heroes."

It was reasonable. "But why would she immediately want him to die?"

Mike shrugged, supplying, "She's stuck in a marriage where she hates her husband in a time divorce wasn't a thing."

I nodded, mulling it over. It wasn't a terrible idea. It still furthered the plot. And it was accurate for that time, especially in noble families. Game of Thrones taught me that. "Ok," I agreed. "We can do that." He visibly relaxed. Oddly, it made me a little less tense too.

I gestured to the computers, and he motioned for me to lead the way. I grabbed the marked-up chapter and made my way to a free computer with a free chair next to it. I settled in, and Mike settled in next to me as if completely natural as I booted up the computer, flash drive at the ready. I opened the chapter file and opened the marked-up chapter and started making the changes.

"So, I felt some real rage coming off the pages with this chapter," Mike stated, taking a sip of his coffee, trying his best to seem nonchalant. "Is everything ok?"

I shrugged, "Yeah. Why not?" I could feel him giving me a weird look, as if he were trying to figure something out. I did my best not to acknowledge it. But his stare persisted. "What?"

"Nothing," he muttered, looking away with a slight blush. "It's just, the past couple times we've met, you've seemed kinda tense." He paused, and I let the silence hang between us, until he leaned forward and said, "You know, if there's something wrong, you can tell me."

I grit my teeth as I typed.

"If it's having to spend so much time with m..."

"It's not that," I cut him off, pulling my hands from the keyboard, chewing on my lower lip. "I mean, yes it is, but not how you think." Now he was confused. I didn't look at him as I confessed, "It's Hudson. He's acting like I'm cheating on him by going to these meetings, which is stupid. Right?"

Mike didn't say anything.

"So, we've been arguing about that. But you know what's even more stupid? When we got together, he was the one who didn't want to be official, because labels were for normies." I was rambling, and barely noticed the frown Mike was giving me. Like he was angry or perplexed. "And he's been talking about our relationship behind my back to our buddies. Aimee completely blindsided me with that the other day." I rolled my eyes. "I mean, is it too much to ask for some trust and privacy in a relationship?"

"N-no," Mike replied, a little nervously.

"NO! Thank you!" I huffed, still steamed from Hudson's recent behavior. I went back to typing furiously, as I gave a semi-laugh, "As if I'd even cheat on him. With you nonetheless!"

Mike took another sip, and this time I did notice his blushing. It was kind of nice to know I could catch him off-guard like that.

"No offense," I offered. Usually, I'd razz him about it, but I decided against it. He was one of the few friends I had that seemed to be on my side with all this Hudson bull. The way Aimee brought it up yesterday sounded like she was trying to convince me to cut-off all communication to Mike, which wasn't going to happen. I needed an A in this class. If that meant working with vanilla Mike for a month, then I would do that. I was enough of an adult to look past the things that annoyed me about him. To be honest, I didn't notice them all that much anymore really.

"None taken," he mumbled awkwardly. There was silence between us as I continued to type. My fingernails tacking against the keyboard was the only noise around us for a minute. "What did you mean, 'labels were for normies?'"

"Oh," I breathed out. "Hudson isn't technically my boyfriend, because he didn't think we should label what we have."

"Riiiiight." The word was long and full of skepticism. I was just as skeptical too when we started, but

I let it go because I loved him. At least, I think I loved him.

Mike didn't push it, so I didn't argue it.

#CarTrouble

He stayed silent as I finished the edits and posted the chapter onto the blog. It was almost 11:30 by the time I was done. I let out a sigh as I stretched, cracking my knuckles. "There we go," I said in a grunt, rolling my neck to stretch. I felt a glorious pop, and my face relaxed.

"There we go," Mike repeated softly. He moved to grab his bag as I grabbed mine, fishing for my keys. Always good to have on hand.

"So, what's the plan for the break?" I asked as I moved to leave, knowing we'd be going the same way. We always parked in the same parking lot.

He shrugged. "Well, I have the schedule set that we will each post three chapters over break week, and you will post the final chapter just after." I nodded along. "Then the first Thursday back, we present our novel."

"It's hard to believe we're already almost done."

"Eh, two thirds. But yes, it is kind of weird we'll be finished next week." He paused before he asked, "Do you have any plans for the break?"

I pursed my lips before replying, "Not really. Just going home and surviving the family reunion."

"Sounds fun," he laughed as we neared my car. I could have sworn I saw a funny look in his eyes as we got close to it, but I couldn't quite put my finger on it. "Well, Rebel, it's been fun." He stuck out his hand for a handshake.

I looked at the hand a little oddly. This was goodbye, I realized. I grasped it, feeling a little inexplicably sad. "For one of us, at least," I joked.

"Probably Professor Harris," he joked back, smirking.

"Probably," I laughed, again feeling inexplicably sad at seeing his smile. It was that moment I realized I'd been holding his hand for too long, and let it go awkwardly, gesturing to my '98 Geo Prizm. "I should go."

"Yeah," he breathed just as awkwardly, putting his well shook hand in his pocket.

He moved towards his car as I hopped in mine. I did catch his eyes on mine for a split second as I went to start my car. The engine revved and then sputtered out. I tried again, and again the car did not come alive. "Oh no. You do not do this to me!" I growled at it as I tried again. Nothing.

Knock Knock

I jumped as I saw Mike standing at my window. I gave him a scowl as he asked, "Car trouble?"

I didn't want to tell him yes. I tried again, but the car was dead. I sat back, hitting my head against the headrest. "Yes," I sighed.

He opened my door and gestured for me to step out. I frowned at him speculatively. "Look, it's about to rain. I'll give you a ride home. You can call Triple A in the morning."

What a gentleman. "You don't have to ..."

"I insist," he said, still holding the door open. "It's late, and I can't just leave you here without a phone."

I frowned, chewing on my bottom lip. He had a point.

Before I could say no, thunder sounded over head just as a droplet of rain hit my windshield. I guess my answer was made for me. "Yeah, ok," I huffed, grabbing my purse and stepping out of the car. A couple loud droplets hit the pavement, rushing me. I quickly locked the Prizm and followed Mike over to his car just as the skies opened up to a torrential downpour. I tried to hop in quickly, but at the first tug on his passenger door, it was locked. "Shit!" I cursed to myself as Mike opened the door for me. I got in, shaking myself free of water. I was already semi-soaked, and my hair was starting to drip and curl. Great.

Another lightning strike nearby flashed as Mike hopped into the driver's seat, growling, "Jeez!" His hair was wetter than mine now, and a bang or two fell away from his usual styling into his verdant eyes. "Sorry about that," he laughed good-naturedly.

I'm not sure what it was. Maybe the wet hair and the rain droplets decorating his face, but his eyes seemed greener, his lips kissably pinker, and his teeth perfect and white. And I felt a sudden urge to see how he tasted. A sharp attraction for him for a brief moment.

His eyes caught mine, and I realized I was staring. I turned quickly, doing my best to hide my blushing as I wrung my hair.

He didn't mention anything, turning to stare out the windshield. "Well," he said coughing awkwardly. A moment of silence hung between us as rain pelted the glass before Mike started up the car. He shifted into drive, then asked, "Where am I dropping you off?"

"Oh," I sputtered, realizing we had never traded that information before. Probably for good reason. "I'm at the corner of Cary and Belvidere."

"Alright," he said blankly with a nod as he drove out of the parking lot toward my apartment. We were silent the whole ride. And I was thankful.

As he pulled into the complex, I saw a familiar crème mini cooper sitting in front of our apartment. "What's Aimee doing here?" I asked blankly as Mike pulled into a parking spot. I don't know why, but with Hudson talking about our relationship to Aimee earlier, I was a little skeptical about her being there. They were probably shit-talking me some more.

I reached for Mike's wrist, feeling him tense lightly underneath me as I said, "Wait for me for a minute."

"O-okay," he replied shakily.

I hopped out, running through the rain to the door. I unlocked the door quietly, so as to not draw attention to myself. If they were talking shit, I wanted to hear what they were saying. I quietly shut the door, only to be greeted with the sounds of the apartment. And Aimee and Hudson. And they *weren't* talking.

"Oh! Oh... OH!" she moaned as I walked into the apartment. Not that I was moving of my own volition. My mind was in too much shock, but my body seemed to take that as keep walking towards the noise. The living room was littered with clothes. His jeans. Her top.

His bedroom door was open, and the angle where I stood, I saw Aimee gripping the edge of the bed, her mouth wide as she moaned and her eyes screwed shut. The way her hair moved with her body, she was clearly getting pounded from behind.

And I was frozen in place.

"OH! HUDSON!!!" she cried out, her voice raspy. "I-I I'm cummi-" She trailed off as a scream tore from her throat.

"Fuck. Aimee." Hudson moaned. The pounding got harder, and then slowed as they groaned, cumming together.

I was going to be sick.

Aimee let out a steadying breath and opened her eyes. The euphoric haze in her gaze lasted a second as her eyes found mine, only to be replaced by horror. I must have looked like a fish out of water, mouth agape and bug-eyed. "Oh fuck. Rebel," she breathed, moving awkwardly off the bed.

I was already bolting for the door.

Before I could even register what was going on, I was back in Mike's car. "What the ...?" he started.

"Drive. Just drive."

#Coming2Terms

If you had told me a month ago I'd be sitting in Gwar Bar, drinking a beer, crying, and spilling my guts to Mike Davis, I'd have said you were insane. Hell, if you would have told me Mike Davis, hater of Romeo and Juliet and all things romantic, would be my knight in shining armor after finding out Hudson was banging my gay best girl-friend ... sorry, bi bestfriend, I'd have said you were insane.

Mike watched me sob into my third beer. I'd been crying since Mike had pulled away after seeing Aimee run out after me in nothing but sheets, and Hudson shirtless behind her. And I mean ugly crying. Big frowny lips. Red, puffy, squinting eyes. Snot. The whole shebang.

I didn't have to explain the situation to him. I was thankful for that. I could just sob into my beer as I mourned my relationship. I moved to take another sip, only to find I'd reached the bottom again. I dropped it, crying into my hands.

Mike waved down a waiter and said, "We'll have another round, and some cheese fries to share."

The waiter nodded and left quickly with a small glance to myself. I chose to ignore it.

It didn't take that long for the food and beers to come back, and I immediately grabbed my bottle and started to sip it. Sip might be an understatement. Guzzle might be more accurate. You know what don't judge. I'm going through some shit right now.

"Ok," Mike started, eyeing me carefully, "slow down."

"I can't," I said through sniffles and gulps. "If I slow down, I start to feel. And I can't feel right now. I just won't be able to handle it."

Mike pursed his lips before stating, "Ok. But what is the plan for tonight? I'm fairly certain you aren't going back to your apartment."

I froze. I hadn't thought about that. "Uhm."

"Do you have a friend's you can go to?"

I tapped the rim of my bottle. "Well, you see," I started, feeling the lump forming again in my throat. I cleared it as best I could, "the closest friend I have on campus ..." I paused before correcting, "*had* on campus was the one fucking my..." I couldn't finish the sentence before falling apart again.

That was the hardest part about this. It wasn't Hudson. I partially expected it from him. It wasn't the first time he cheated on me technically. The first time I had forgiven him because he'd gotten drunk after a bad argument, and had a one night stand. Aimee had known about that though. She knew how it almost broke us. How it hurt me. That was the biggest betrayal. Not Hudson. Aimee.

Mike let out a sigh, putting his bottle down. He'd been drinking a non-alcoholic beer, being the DD for the night. "Well, my roommates are gone on break, so my place is free." I stared at him wide-eyed, trying to calm down my sniffles. Did he just offer to take me to his place? A part of me was floored, while the other part of me was curious.

I nodded, doing my best to dry my eyes. "Yes," I said. Not like the night could get any worse.

#TruthorDare

It was almost midnight when we got to Mike's apartment and still pouring. We ran to the door, Mike guiding me carefully because the beers had begun to hit, and the floor sometimes moved beneath me.

He fumbled with his keys, but got the door open, saying a small, "Here we go," as he guided me in, and assisted me in finding his couch. He let out an awkward sigh as I sat down with a slump and a giggle. Yeah, I was toasted, but I'd been way worse before.

"You aren't going to drink?" I asked. It came out normal to me, but Mike grinned as if I'd asked something funny.

"I think you're drunk enough for the both of us," he commented.

I frowned. "I don't feel comfortable being the only one drunk. You might take advantage of me."

He raised an eyebrow at the last remark. "I'm sorry, but you'll find I am a perfect gentleman."

"Pfft." The sound wasn't pretty or graceful. And I threw myself forward as I made it, almost falling off the couch. "No such thing."

He shrugged.

"Please," I stated. "I feel like I'm being judged."

He rolled his eyes, getting up and walking to the fridge. He held up a six pack of craft beer, and I raised an eyebrow. I didn't take him for a craft beer man. I would have put money down that he was a Budweiser or bust kind of man. He popped off the top easily, and took a swig as he walked back to the couch, setting the rest of the pack on the counter.

I moved the beer package around to see the label. It wasn't a beer I recognized. "Hmm," I grunted in spite of myself.

"What?" he asked.

"I didn't take you for a craft man."

He nodded. "Jo and I talked about starting our own brew. Both of us are into hoppier beers, but Jo is kind of a mad scientist when it comes to flavors. Like mint & barley beer."

I shrugged. "Sounds delicious actually." I wasn't lying. Barley would deliver the hops, while mint might just give the beer a cool lift. I snuggled into the couch with a sigh. "So what else aren't you telling me, Mr. Craft Beer?"

He frowned with a shrug. "It's not like I've been purposefully holding back. What do you want to know?"

I reached forward and grabbed another beer, popping the tab off and taking a sip. Mike eyed me carefully, and something about the way his green eyes fell on me ... maybe it was the alcohol talking to me, but I really didn't want him looking anywhere else tonight. I tipped my drink to him before taking a sip, and as it hit my tongue, my eyes flew wide at the taste. Definitely hoppy. I could see Mike grinning at me amusedly, so I did my best to brush it off as I swallowed.

I cleared my throat, then started, "Why don't we play a round of Truth or Dare, just to get to know each other a bit."

He let out a small snort. "Ok."

"So," I said, straightening up. "Truth or Dare, Mike?"

"Truth."

I narrowed my gaze, looking around the room, before I asked, "What's your favorite movie?"

He pursed his lips. "That one's tough." He chewed on the inside of his cheek before answering, "I've got three that I love equally." He held up three fingers. "12 Angry Men. It's raw and really good storytelling. The Godfather, because Coppola is a legend and Marlon Brando is iconic as Vito Corleone. And lastly The Princess Bride. I laugh every time I watch it, and I know every line."

I raised my eyebrows at that. All really good picks. And here I was expecting him to say Suicide Squad or some shit.

"Your turn, Rebel. Truth or Dare?"

I narrowed my gaze with an impish smile. "Dare."

He raised an eyebrow at me. "I dare you to tell my why you write."

I rolled my eyes. "You can't dare someone to tell the truth."

He shrugged, with a sip and a smile. "Sure you can."

"No, Dare means I've got to do something," I huffed at him. Good-naturedly. I was having a good time.

He rolled his eyes. "Fine. I dare you to put on some music. Something good."

I frowned. "I don't have my iPod or phone, so..."

He reached in his pocket, pulling out his phone and flipping to a radio app. There were Bluetooth speakers the phone was already hooked up to. The song that came up was one I recognized. One I loved.

He leaned back with a smile and a small sigh, "I love this song." My eyes went wide. "It always reminds me of fall, just as it's turning to winter. It's my favorite time of year."

I smirked at him, "You mean now?"

He shrugged. "Yeah. But like camping in fall. Watching the leaves turn." He gave me a calm smile as he asked, "What about you?"

"Well, I liked the song, but I feel like on principle I have to hate it now," I replied, kind of mournfully.

He gave me a weird look. "Why?"

"Because it's mainstream. Especially if someone like you likes it," I answered.

Now he was frowning, and I knew I said it wrong. "What do you mean by someone like me?"

"I mean," I started, gesticulating at him, "if you like it, probably everyone likes it, meaning for the band it's all about making money rather than the art. So, it's shallow to like it."

Now he looked baffled, and I knew I'd really put my foot in it. "Are you saying I'm shallow?"

"No," I sighed. I shook my head quickly, which only made me dizzy. Bad move. "Look, I'm drunk and everything is coming out wrong."

"Ok, then what's wrong with artists who find success in their art?" he asked.

"It's not that," I argued. "It's the machine of it. The system." He gave a small "Ah." I could tell he disagreed with me on some level, maybe all of it. But I didn't care. What was new? Our relationship was built on argumentative bullshit. "Anyway, it's my turn." His green gaze found mine again, and my heart skipped a beat. I swallowed hard before asking, "Truth or Dare?"

"Truth."

"Why do you write?"

He smiled slyly at me. "Thief."

"Answer the question," I goaded, taking a sip of my beer.

He chewed on his lip, looking away guiltily before answering, "I'm not sure I want to tell you."

"Tsk tsk. You gotta' answer."

He let out a laugh at my excited expression, as he said, "Fine. I started writing in High School originally to get a girl." I laughed, and he rolled his eyes as he added, "She was totally out of my league, but she had a thing for creative types. But she was never into me, so I kept writing to escape my feelings. Then a teacher saw some of my writings, and told me it was good enough to publish. Then I started just doing it for fun."

I was hooked with his story, totally hanging off every word. "So, what happened to the girl?"

He shrugged. "Last I heard she's at NYU getting a degree in acting." He shot me a look, as if curious about something before he added, "I'm not into her anymore, if that's what you're wondering."

I looked at him innocently. I wasn't thinking that. I also wasn't thinking that I was happy to hear he wasn't hung up on some high school crush.

"Your turn. Truth or Dare?"

"Truth," I answered quickly.

"Why would you settle for a guy like Hudson?" he asked. I raised my eyebrows at him, as if asking was kind of dangerous territory. "I mean you're pretty, smart, and talented. That's kind of the trifecta. There's gotta' be others trying to be with you."

"No, there isn't," I stated, setting my jaw. He looked at me weirdly as I answered, "I've been told I'm intimidating."

"Then you're asking for the wrong guys," he said. And the way he looked in my eyes, it felt as if he really looked at me. He didn't see me as intimidating. I was a challenge. I also hadn't noticed when he'd gotten so close to me. I could smell his aftershave, even though it smelled like a natural musk.

"Your turn," I breathed, holding his verdant gaze. The air between us was electric. "Truth or Dare."

"Dare."

A stupid fantasy came to my head. I decided to run with it. "I dare you to kiss me."

Before I could do anything, his lips were on mine, feverishly pulling me to him. His kiss was like nothing I'd ever experienced before, and I wanted more.

#XOXO

It was so strange. In a good way. Kissing him made my body feel alive for the first time in a long time. My hands easily found their way into his hair, which was still damp from the rain, and God damn was it sexy. He had one hand cradling the back of my skull, making sure it was supported, and his other hand was on my hip, kneading it like fresh dough. The sensations of just his fingers on me was enough to realize I really had been settling. Hudson had never kissed me like this.

Hell. *No one* had ever kissed me like this.

His tongue licked at my lips, begging for entrance, and I accepted. His first delve into my mouth was cautious and curious, but once his tongue met mine, it was a battle for dominance. It was incredibly sexy, and I won't lie, I was getting incredibly turned on by his skills on display. My lack of recent sex could have added to that, but it was like Mike not only knew how to work his tongue perfectly against mine, but it was like he was born for it.

He eased me down on the couch, which was way more comfortable for the both of us. Him between my legs as we made out, his fingers touching my body so lovingly. It was intoxicating. More so than the beer.

He was hard. I could tell. I could feel his mass through my jeans. And my body ached for it.

With one of my legs curled on his hip, I tried to leverage for more friction. I just needed to be touched, desperately. "Please," I moaned.

"Please ... what?" he asked in between tantalizing kisses.

"Touch me," I begged, my hips drawing up to his again. A part of me couldn't believe I was asking Mike this, but the overwhelming majority of my mind wanted him playing with me until I finally came.

He paused a second, looking deep into my eyes. That gaze of his was so fuckable right now. "I don't want to do anything you'll regret."

Quickly, I unfastened my jeans, inching them down before grabbing his hand. "I wouldn't be asking if I didn't want it."

I barely saw the small nod he gave, letting his hand be guided into my curls by my own hand. My breath hitched as I felt his fingers ghost over my sensitive folds. He spread the lips so his fingers could nestle in between them, and again I let out inadvertent moan. He dipped one finger in, then two, each pumping in and out. His thumb found my clit, rubbing small circles in it, sending shots of ecstasy into my stomach where I felt its pressure growing. I let out a pleasure filled gasp, and my eyes rolled upward.

This was amazing. Who would have thought Vanilla Mike would have been the one to make me sound like a porn star.

I felt his mouth on me again, this time trailing down my neck to my chest. I wanted out of my t-shirt so he could kiss and feel more of my body with his glorious hands.

The music cutoff for a second as his phone started vibrating. I felt his fingers inside me slow as he looked up. "Keep going!" I urged, desperately grabbing at the phone. It stopped ringing, and he did as I bid.

I was bucking against his hand now, crying out, "Yes! Mike! Right there. Right there!" His fingers moved quickly as I felt the pressure crack and burst. A mind shattering orgasm shot through me, and I made incoherent moans as I clutched at him.

My mind felt hazy as I looked up at Mike, seeing his verdant eyes grinning back at me. He wasn't breathing nearly as hard as I was. I shuddered as I felt him pull his fingers out of me, his hand out of my pants.

"That's enough for tonight. I need to see who called," he breathed easing off me.

"I'll be ready for more in a minute," I offered.

He smiled, grabbing his phone. As he looked at the screen, his face fell to a frown.

"What?" I asked, starting to sit up a little.

He showed me the screen, and it showed an ongoing phone call with my cellphone. I scowled, knowing exactly who it was.

I grabbed the phone from Mike, who stood walking into the kitchen, trying to give me a semblance of privacy, his hands in his pockets. I put the phone to my ear as I set my jaw. "Did you enjoy the show, Hudson?"

"How could you, Reb?" his voice broke as he asked it. A part of me was a little proud of it. "With him!?"

"How could *you*, Hudson, *with Aimee!*" I screamed the last part into the phone. There was silence on the other end as I added venomously, "You better be gone by the time I get there tomorrow. I don't want to see either of your fucking faces anymore! WE'RE DONE!" I hung up the phone and threw it to the other end of the couch.

Zen yoga breathing. Deep breath in, slow release. Repeat.

All I wanted was to lose myself. Forget tonight ever happened ... well some of it. I turned to Mike, who was still standing awkwardly in the kitchen with his hands in his pockets. I sent him a pained, but trying to be flirty, smile as I asked, "What about you and I head to bed?" My intention was clear.

"Ok," he said, "you can take my room." He pointed a side door behind the TV wall. "I'll sleep on the couch tonight."

I let out a scoff, eyeing him weirdly. "You don't want to ..."

"Not tonight," he answered quickly, and I could see in his eyes there was no convincing him otherwise, which confused me. It was my understanding if a woman was ready and willing, most men jumped on that. And I could see he was still hard. The bulge in his jeans was still significant. "I could," he added, "but it wouldn't be right."

I stood, blinking in my confusion. Was this rejection? It wasn't like I hadn't been told no to sex before. But I'd never had a night where I got off, and the guy was ok with leaving it there. Hudson always acted like if I got off, even minimally, he was owed an ejaculation. Maybe my limited experience was jading my understanding. Hudson had been the only guy I'd ever banged before.

"Ok..." I muttered, still utterly confounded by what just happened. This whole night was fucking with my head, especially Mike and his magic hands, making me wonder what other parts of his body were magic.

Maybe I would never know. Mike was still Mike. A guy I loved to hate until about two weeks ago. That was a terrible basis for a relationship. I was still a little shocked that I let him touch me in that way. Probably more shocked that I enjoyed it, wanted more of it.

"Ok ..." I said again, in a bit of a daze as I walked to the bedroom he'd offered. I opened the door to find it spotless. His walls were sparsely decorated except for a Far Side calendar, and a poster for a more popular Indie Rock band I'd never really given a chance. There was a TV on the far wall with a gaming system hooked up, next to closed closet doors. A full-size bed with a muted patchwork quilt was pushed against the window in the corner next to a bookshelf filled to the brim with books.

Most of them were classics I recognized. Heart of Darkness, The Scarlet Letter, Paradise Lost, The Divine Comedy, Frankenstein. I was surprised to see several works by Shakespeare, remembering his abhorrence for Romeo and Juliet. He had Macbeth, Hamlet, Othello, and Much Ado About Nothing, and a book of all his sonnets. Intrigued, I pulled out the sonnets, seeing several bookmarks placed in it. I opened to one of the later ones he'd marked, finding sonnet 127. I saw his notes on the side, and his underlining throughout the text. In the corner he wrote, "First of the dark lady." He also noted in another corner, "Societal standards of beauty are bullshit."

I let out a small chuckle, seeing he'd given the note an asterisk. I read through the poem quickly and my smile grew.

I'm sorry.

I'm really sorry.

Rebel, please talk to me.

I didn't mean for that to happen.

Rebel, please.

I'm so so sorry.

My phone buzzed again, and I looked at it, seeing another text message from Aimee.

Happy Thanksgiving.

I rolled my eyes and hit ignore. I should have blocked her number. I really should have. I don't know. A part of me felt bad about doing that though.

Aimee had been my best friend for the past few years. My closest confidant. And all of a sudden she was supposed to be neither. She was the other woman. I couldn't understand for the life of me how this girl who constantly preached about how women needed to stick together and about our close sisterhood would betray another woman like that. Hell, not even that. How she could betray me like that.

Since the break started, I hadn't even thought of Hudson really. I'd blocked him on all of my social media, phone, email. Everything. As far as technology went, Hudson didn't even exist. As for our shared living situation, I moved out, broke my lease and packed up my stuff, all of which I brought home as I tried to figure out my new living situation. I still had exams and several more semester to go before graduation.

No. It was Aimee and Mike I couldn't stop thinking about. Aimee because she'd fucked Hudson. And Mike because we had this amazing moment, and then pretty much radio silence. The morning after, he'd helped me with my car situation, but that was it. He didn't want to talk about the night before, short of the email notifications when his chapters were posted, there was nothing. And I didn't know how to feel about that.

"Something up?" Lucy asked quietly, leaning towards me to keep the rest of the table out of the conversation as we ate Thanksgiving Dinner. She'd just gotten in late in the night before, so I hadn't been able to fill her in on everything that had happened.

I gave her a pursed smile before replying, "It's not really good dinner conversation." I looked across the table at our parents and grandparents who had joined us, as well as our divorced Aunt and her two boys, both of which were still in middle school, and gushing over the new super hero movie.

Lucy frowned, clearly resolving to get it out of me later.

"So, Lucy," our grandfather started with a smile. "What are you up to recently."

Lucy smiled beamingly. "Oh, I got a job at a firm in Richmond. So, I'll be near Reb." She nudged her elbow at me, shooting me an excited smile.

I perked up quickly while the family congratulated her. "Really? When?"

She looked at me curiously. "I move into the new apartment tomorrow, and start Monday. They want me well trained before busy season." Now I was grinning, and her expression grew even more curious.

"Sweet!" I cheered. Now she was eyeing me carefully. I never used "Sweet" unless I wanted something. When the rest of the family had moved onto another topic, I leaned over to her. "I really need to talk to you after dinner."

Lucy frowned, before looking to Mom. "Hey, Mom, may Reb and I be excused?" Before Mom could answer, Lucy grabbed my wrist with a Cheshire cat grin, dragging me upstairs. We walked into her old bedroom, and she shut the door, crossing her arms. "Ok, spill."

I huffed, slightly slouching at her insistence. I gave a small eyeroll before opening, "Alright, so you know how I went in on a lease with the guy I was seeing last year?"

Lucy's gaze narrowed on me. She had the same dark eyes I did, but her face was a little rounder like our mother's, framed by her strawberry blonde locks. "I remember Mom and Dad advising you against going in on a lease with a guy, saying it would blow up in your face."

I didn't look at her. I didn't need to be reminded I was a romantic idiot last year, thinking Hudson was everything. I'd already been kicking myself all week because of my stupidity.

Lucy now looked at me with curious pity. "What happened?"

"Well," I started, doing my best to put on a brave face, "it blew up in my face."

She walked over, putting and arm around me as I spilled everything that happened. The project with Mike. Hudson's jealousy. Finding Hudson with Aimee. My official dumping and blocking of Hudson. As well as the rather quick hookup with Mike, leaving me confused.

She gave a small frown as she asked, "Why does 'Mike Davis' sound familiar?"

"You probably heard me ranting about him last semester. His critique of my short story was ... it ripped my story to shreds, essentially," I replied.

"Ah," Lucy said with an understanding smile. When I had shown her the short story back in May, she had agreed with his assessment that it was a poem and not a short story, and I didn't talk to her for a week. "So, after working together on this project, you want to be with him?"

"I never said that," I said quickly.

Lucy gave me a confused look with a small shake of her head. "I'm sorry. It just seems like you've got a thing him."

I blushed. "I do not have a thing for Mike Davis. It was a one-night hand job."

"Ri-ight," Lucy laughed, looking at me as if she knew my mind better than I knew it.

"I'm serious," I said. "I don't even think he wants to talk to me after we turn in the project." I realized how that sounded, and I added quickly, "And that's *fine*. It was a one-time thing."

Lucy still smiled knowingly. "Whatever." She stood with a small sigh. "You can move in with me tomorrow on one condition."

"What?"

"You tell Mom and Dad why you're no longer leasing with Hudson," she stated, her arms crossed, and her expression stern.

I gave her a small pout. Anything but that.

I was surfing the internet on my laptop. It was almost midnight, and the only illumination in my room was the laptop's screen. Everything had been squared away. I'd confessed to my parents that they were right about Hudson, and that I'd be moving in with Lucy the next day. They'd been oddly supportive.

They didn't need me to go into detail. I just told them that Hudson and I broke up, and that it was bad. And I was thankful that's all they needed to hear.

I heard a notification ding on both my phone and computer, and I looked.

Mike Davis: Final Chapter posted

The email sent a wave of uncertainty through me. A small sense of sadness.

I pulled up our blog and read:

The fog lingered around the graveyard, clinging to the ground as it rolled over the earth. Curling around mossy headstones and time worn statues. This was her resting place. The name Capulet had been engraved on the marble mausoleum long before. Even though she'd married, and her name now Montague, the Capulet tomb was to be her final home. She hadn't been Montague long enough to warrant a spot in their vault.

The page stood, careful eye out over the graveyard. He shook a little with fear. His eyes caught moving shadows, and he let out a howl.

Paris hadn't even made it into Juliet's tomb, and came running back as soon as his page called. "What?" Paris hissed.

Page gestured to the moving shadows. "I saw something."

Paris stepped closer.

"Balthazar," a voice called. Paris knew who it was immediately. Romeo. "Hand me the crowbar."

Balthazar looked to his friend and master, handing him the crowbar as he clutched the pickaxe. "Why are we here?"

Romeo gripped the crowbar tightly before answering, "I missed the funeral. I wish to pay my respects." He placed the crowbar first, then pointed to where the pickaxe was to be place. "But mainly it's to retrieve her jewelry. It's better I have it than some grave robber."

Balthazar nodded gravely in agreement.

Romeo held up a hand, saying, "Also, please do not bother me. Some things should remain private between a husband and his bride."

Balthazar frowned, but gave an affirming nod, helping him with the tomb's seal. Once it was opened, Balthazar stepped aside.

As Romeo's attendant left, Paris jumped up. "Fiend! Theif!"

Romeo looked at him tiredly. "Paris" he sighed. "Why are you here?"

"I'm here to make sure my Juliet's tomb isn't disturbed," Paris answered. "And look what I've found! Romeo robbing her grave!"

Romeo frowned, "She was never **your** Juliet!"

Paris gripped at his sword, shaking with rage. *"I loved her! I wanted to marry her!"*

"Her family chose me," he stated darkly. He gripped at his sword lightly. *"But if it's a fight you want, then have at thee, boy!"*

Paris launched at him, sword glistening in the moonlight. Romeo parried quickly. Paris's page ran as they fought. With a quick move, Romeo disarmed him, but Paris lunged at him with a punch, and almost instinctually, Romeo drove his sword through him. He felt the warmth of the blood on his hands. He heard Paris cough, blood dribbling down his lip.

He laid him down, removing his sword and cleaning it. *"I'm sorry."*

"Please. Lay me next to Juliet," Paris coughed. *"Lay me next to my love."*

Romeo frowned, looking back to the opened tomb. Paris had been with someone, so he would need to be quick before that someone brought more men. *"I will put you to rest,"* he promised. Paris's head fell to the side. He'd passed.

Romeo picked up his body, carrying him into the tomb. He placed him on the ground in some distant corner, before looking into the Capulet's tomb, finding her.

She looked as radiant in death as she had in life. He walked towards her, pulling the shroud from her body. The sight took his breath away. Made it all seem too real.

There she lay, eyes closed, lips parted as if sleeping soundly. There was still some red in her lips and cheeks. Her hair had been styled in lose ringlets and adorned with white flowers. "Oh, Juliet," Romeo sighed, his hand drifting to move one tendril of hair. "Why are you still so beautiful? I'd hoped a better future for us. One not so steeped in death. There lies Tybalt in his bloody sheet, and Paris here as well."

He knelt next to her, studying her face carefully, hoping this was a trick. It would be like her to do such a thing. He reached for her hand, and it felt as cold as the tomb.

"I would've chosen a brighter path, I think. I'm told this was your own design. I think I understand." It was hard to keep the emotions from his words. He felt like he failed, utterly and completely. He gave a small sniffle before adding, "I'd hoped we could get over our differences for our families' sake. Start anew with happy hope.

"But that was never going to happen. We were too different. Too volatile a pair. Who could have ever thought that we could fix what was never made to fit."

His grip tightened on her hand, as he felt the first tear fall from his eyes. Even though they had hated each other, he'd never wanted her to be here. He dried his eyes and leaned over to give her forehead a chaste kiss. "Sleep well, dear Juliet. May heaven treat you better than Earth."

When he pulled away to look at his wife one last time, he was met with the chocolaty brown gaze of her, still alive with her ever present fiery spirit.

That was it.

That was it?

I didn't understand. We'd agreed that Romeo was there to make sure Juliet was dead. To finish the job himself.

Then why was he so sad? Why was he talking about hoping for a better future between them? I read it again to see if I missed anything. Then another time to make sure.

The only thing I could think of was that Mike wanted to change the ending. But why?

That was when I realized it. My back straightened as the thought came clearly to my head.

Quickly I began to write. I had all weekend to do it, and I'd be moving in the morning. But the chapter just flowed out of me and onto the page. The book needed an ending. Mike needed an answer.

#FreshStart

Lucy's new apartment was rather industrial looking, in a very currently popular way. The ceiling were very high and made of original wood. Some of the walls were exposed old brick. And the windows were large, almost bay. It was clear someone had done a lot of remodeling on these apartments, as everything else looked brand new. From the kitchens, to the bathrooms, to the bedrooms.

I was lucky Lucy had gotten a two-bedroom apartment, hoping to find a roommate at her new office. Now she had me to take up the spare room. It took us most of the morning to get the furniture in and set up. The rest of the day I spent fixing my room, getting my clothes put away, hanging decorations, setting up my writing desk with my laptop, typewriter, cutesy desk lamp, and pencil holder.

On Saturday, I got another text from Aimee, asking to meet for coffee, and I finally agreed to it. I sat at the coffee shop we'd agreed on. A coffee shop we used to go to all the time. I'd ordered my standard. Mocha latte. I wasn't in the mood for pumpkin today.

I was halfway through my coffee when I saw Aimee come into the coffee shop. I bristled a little when I saw her gaze find mine, quickly looking away. But this was something I had to do. Something I had to hear.

Aimee sat across from me. I grabbed at my coffee, refusing to look at her. The memory of her moans was still so clear. "You not gonna' get some coffee?"

She cleared her throat carefully. "No."

I took a sip, savoring the silence. A part of me didn't want to be here. You can understand.

After a minute of nothing, Aimee asked, "Did you enjoy your Thanksgiving?"

"I really don't want to talk about my break," I said, my gaze finally cutting into hers.

"Ok."

There was another long beat of silence before she asked, "What do you want to talk about?"

My jaw tensed before I answered, "How about you and Hudson?"

Her blue eyes saddened. "You really want to know?" she asked.

"It's the only reason I'm here."

"Ok," Aimee sighed, grabbing a lock of her perfect blond hair and twirling it between two fingers nervously. "Well, the first time it happened was totally by accident." I frowned at her. How do you *accidentally* fuck someone? My point exactly. And don't think I missed the part where she said "the first time." "We were totally drunk. He just had a fight with you, at least that's what he told me. But when we woke in the morning, I told him never again." But we both knew that wasn't the end of the story.

"When was that?" I asked carefully.

"Back in June," Aimee breathed cautiously. She could see my lividity in my gaze. She was the one-night stand Hudson had finally confessed to after weeks of gaslighting. So many weeks past, both of them telling me I was seeing things between them that weren't there. When Hudson finally confessed, I felt vindicated, and let it go. Clearly that was my mistake.

"I know. I'm sorry," she said quickly. I didn't say anything as she continued. "We didn't do anything for a long time after that! I swear! I hated knowing I was the one who had caused you to hurt so much. It killed me to even think about it." She took a shuddering sigh and even a glistening tear. My my, she truly knew how to pull at the heart strings.

Not that my heart was moved in the slightest, though.

"But, I don't know, something happened. After summer break, he told me about how much he missed me and wanted to be with me. He said he was staying with you because you'd both signed a lease, and he couldn't back out. But that he loved me.

"I believed him. I still do. I think I'm in love with him, and it killed me to think I could never tell you how I felt."

My stomach churned at her story, my mind seething with rage. I could feel the pressure of my teeth grinding together as my jaw tightened with each revelation. I knew I was probably sneering at her confession.

"I never wanted you to find out like that. Neither of us did. We had a plan. He was going to ..."

I cut her off as I stood. She could see in my cold frown I was resigned to anything else she had to say. I didn't care about their intentions. Hell, I didn't care if they were fucking soulmates! You just don't do what they did.

"Rebel, please," she started. "I'm so sorry."

"I could get over Hudson lying to me like that," I said, cutting her off again. Her voice now was like listening to nails screeching across chalkboard. And my voice was the only thing silencing hers. "I'd forgiven him the first time, but I'm not an idiot. He knew after the thing June we were done if I'd found out he'd cheated again. I'd told him that much."

My glare settled on her now. I had waterworks of my own, but I wasn't going to use them on her. I was stronger than that. *Better* than that. "But you were my best friend." I saw a tear roll down her cheek as I reiterated, "My best friend."

"Please, Reb," she sniffled.

"Don't," I growled through gritted teeth. I shook my head as I added saying, "I can't forgive what you did. You knew how much it hurt me. You lied to me. Made me think I was crazy for a time. Let's not forget that." I didn't mean for the biting laugh to come out of me at the last part, but it felt cathartic to get it all off my chest.

I saw her lips trembling in a pout, and oddly I didn't pity her.

"You can have him. I don't care," I said with finality. "As far as I'm concerned, you and I are no longer friends."

With that, I grabbed my coffee and left.

#NewBeginnings

"Next group to present their novel is Rebel and Mike," Professor Harris called out.

I'd been looking over at Mike all class, hoping to see him catch my gaze or something. Something to tell me he'd been thinking of me like I'd been thinking of him the last several days. He'd been too engrossed in his notes it seemed.

I quickly stood, only to see Mike stand simultaneously with me. We walked to the front, and Mike pulled up our NaNoWriMo blog while I would address the class. We'd discussed this early on in the project.

"Ok," I started, smiling at the class. "For our NaNoWriMo, _Star-Crossed_, we took Shakespeare's _Romeo and Juliet_, and flipped it on its head to become a dark comedy." This intrigued some people.

"Our word count hit just north of thirty-five thousand words, but we did complete it. So, it's really more of a novella."

Professor Harris marked something down. I tried my best not to notice or freak out about the grade. So we were fifteen thousand short. That didn't mean we didn't finish our book. Plus, it was only five thousand away from being a novel technically.

"It's twenty-four chapters hit all the major points of the original play, which worked perfectly for pacing, because the original play had exactly twenty-four scenes. So, we alternated scenes and viewpoints per chapter, writing from both Romeo's and Juliet's perspectives."

Mike started in this time, stating, "Our story starts with Romeo and Juliet's families arranging for our star-crossed characters to marry, even though Romeo and Juliet hate each other. The story proceeds as the original, except with Romeo and Juliet pining for each other, they are each plotting to kill the other to escape the fate of being married."

There were murmurs through the class, and I quickly added, "Again, dark comedy rather than a tragedy. Questions?"

"Why wouldn't they just divorce?" one of the guys who always sat in the back of the class, and usually smelled heavily of hemp asked.

"It's based during the same time as the original. At the time, historically speaking, divorce wasn't commonly practiced, if at all," Mike stated. He looked around carefully before asking, "Any other questions?"

No one offered.

Professor Harris raised her hand, politely. "Link?"

"The link is available in the class chatroom if anyone wants to read it," I answered, more to the rest of the class. Professor Harris already knew where it was. She'd been keeping tabs on all the novels during the month.

Professor Harris gave a nod, signaling that was the end of the presentation, giving a small congenial applause, which the class joined in with. We went back to our seats as Professor Harris took our spot up front, starting, "Well, that is it for class. Remember, our next two classes are the class survey and then reviewing the final exam study guide. So please, do not miss either one of those!" The class was already packing their bags as she said the last sentence. Most were heading towards the exit as some crowded around Professor Harris to ask questions.

My focus was on Mike, who was already out the door and headed for the parking lot. I slung my bag over my shoulder and ran after him.

He was halfway across the parking lot when I caught up to him, yelling like a crazed woman, "MIKE! MIKE!! WAIT UP!" He froze, hearing me call out to him, turning around with a befuddled frown. I jogged up to him, out of breath. "We need to talk," I said between gasps.

His brow furrowed nervously, over hopeful green eyes. At least they looked hopeful to me. "About what?"

I shot him a scowl, still breathless as I replied, "Oh, you know, that night we made out and got a little handsy. You remember." I waved my fingers in gesture when I mentioned his hands-on participation. Pun intended.

He blushed.

I smiled. He was cute when he blushed.

"So, what happened there?" I asked.

He put his hands in his jean pockets awkwardly before he replied, "Nothing."

I raised a skeptical eyebrow at him as I scoffed, "Nothing? It didn't feel like nothing. Felt actually more like a lot of something."

"Do you want it to be something?" he asked carefully. I frowned. I hated being answered with a question.

"Do you?" He looked away with a blush. I scowled, hating his silence a little more. "I offered sex, remember? *You* were the one who turned it down."

"It's because I'm not a rebound," he said quickly, bristling. His mouth pursed and shoulders dropped. "I'm not the guy who steals some guy's girlfriend. I'm not the guy who takes advantage of a girl's compromised emotions or impaired judgement. I'm just not that guy."

I looked at him shocked, not expecting those answers to come tumbling out of him. His shoulders slumped as he finally looked at me, and his green gaze was sad. "What I did that night bothers me, because for one night, I was that guy."

There was silence between us as I tried to understand what he was saying. He hadn't done anything wrong, yet he felt guilty. Why?

"If it makes you feel any better," I said, "I was never technically Hudson's girlfriend."

"It doesn't," he stated. He closed his eyes as he added, "I really wish that had happened under different circumstances, because I ..." he cut himself off with a resigned huff. He turned on his heel as he shook his head, but I grabbed his arm quickly, and I felt him freeze under my touch.

"Because you actually like me," I said, my grip on him tight. I'm not an idiot. I could tell. He'd been throwing signs as obvious as neon billboards, if I had just taken the time to actually look. "Well, the feeling's mutual."

He turned to me quickly with a frown, as if not entirely certain I was being honest. I laughed at his expression. "Didn't you read the last chapter?" His expression told me he didn't, and I scoffed. I pulled out my phone, reading the last sentence:

As the first rays of sunrise shone, Romeo and Juliet left the tomb, hand in hand, embracing their new destiny together.

The End.

I laughed as I added, "Next time you ask a girl her feelings, maybe read the -"

He cut me off quickly, slamming his mouth into mine. His hands were in my hair, holding my head at the perfect angle for him as his tongue licked at me lips eagerly. I smiled, opening my mouth to him as my arms hung around his neck. A shock went through me as his tongue wrestled against my own. And I couldn't have been happier.

#XRated

Mike pressed me against the apartment door, his lips pressed against mine, kissing me so passionately that my eyes rolled back into my head a little. It had been a week since we presented our project. We'd gone on several dates since then, and Mike had really surprised me. He was incredibly deep, and I was surprised I'd never realized how much. But that's distracting from what was going on now.

I should start with how we got there. It started with a debate over art and meaning and philosophy behind art which got a little heated. It wasn't the first time our dates took a turn like that either. These debates were different from regular arguments though that ended with the two people involved calling the other names. They were solid debates. Sources must be cited. Concessions would be made. And they always ended with laughter a snuggling. It felt healthier, and I'd never realized I was actually good at it.

Our debate was going well, but as soon as I unlocked my apartment door, he cut off one of my points with a kiss. It started out earnestly, but quickly picked up steam. I could feel his fingers kneading through my clothes as his tongue delved into me. I felt his hips press into mine, and my legs shifted open a little. I was ready.

I fumbled with the doorknob, pushing it open, and dragging him inside. I pulled away for a second, my fingers entwining with his as I looked at him. I could see in his eyes he wasn't saying no this time. I smiled, pulling him towards my bedroom door.

I dropped his hands as we walked through, backing towards the bed as I unbuttoned my blouse. "Lock the door," I instructed as I slowly exposed my bra, then my bellybutton. He did so as I dropped my shirt to the ground. He turned back to watch me as I undid my pants, dropping them to the ground as well. He quickly pulled off his shirt, exposing his beautiful chest.

He wasn't super muscular, but perfectly lean.

He was on me again in a second, his hands all over me as his tongue explored my mouth again. His fingers slipped under my underwear to squeeze my ass cheek as he pressed me into the bed. My legs wrapped around his hips, and I felt his engorged penis through his jeans grinding into my already dripping pussy.

I felt his fingers deftly unhook my bra, pulling it away and letting my breasts spill. His mouth traveled down to my collar as his free hand squeezed my boob, the pad of his thumb rubbing circles into my nipple. I let out an ecstatic moan. I needed more.

My hands quickly drifted down, helping him out of his pants, wanting to feel him against me. He wasn't wearing underwear. I grinned, caressing his penis as he kicked off his pants. He let out a grunt, the hand on my ass squeezing tight, before hooking a finger in its hem and dragging them down as he trailed kisses down my body that sent shivers down my spine.

As he knelt over me, his hands on my thighs before spreading my lips wide and delving a finger, then two into me. It already felt amazing as his fingers scissored in me, and then I felt his tongue drag up my vagina to my clit, where his tongue continued to press and circle. My fingers clenched the sheets, feeling the increasing pressure building in my center as his tongue made love to me. God, his tongue was magic, too!

I couldn't keep my hips contained nor my moans as my orgasm got closer and closer to its peak. I felt the pop then release, the endorphins of my orgasm rushing through me as I groaned. I was surprised to feel him stay there, licking up my juices. His tongue still lapped at me lovingly as I came down from the headrush.

He eased himself up, pulling me into another kiss. The taste of me on his lips was oddly intoxicating, and I wanted him all over again.

I rolled us over, pinning him under me, grabbing his member firmly as I guided it into me. He was thick, but not too long, and he slid into me perfectly. I started pumping up and down slowly, grinding into him feeling the climb to my orgasm's peak again. He leaned up, putting his mouth on my nipple as his fingers played with the other. It felt amazing.

The climb stalled for a minute, and he seemed to sense it as he flipped us, pressing into me deeper. I cried out, "Yes! Ah!" as he started pumping into me. The friction of his hips connecting with my clit as his head hit the spot that made me cry out in pleasure. He set in with a rhythm that had me screaming his name in seconds. "Mike! Yes! Fuck YES! Mike! I'm ... I'm gonna ..."

He swallowed my moans with a kiss, his pace quickening until I felt him finish in me, and the pressure of it hurtled me off into my own mind-blowing orgasm.

After a minute of heavy breathing, neither of us moving as we recovered, he slipped out of me, pulling me close as he gave me tender kiss. "You are perfect," he breathed, his arms draped over me.

I smirked. "You're not so bad yourself."

#RudeAwakening

We stayed in each other's arms, comfortably existing between the worlds of wake and slumber. It was warm and soft. I wanted to stay there forever, feeling his body against mine, holding me close.

It was interrupted by a loud banging on the front door of the apartment. I sat up, looking towards the living space with a frown. Who on Earth could that be?

Mike seemed to be thinking the same as me, as he deftly rolled off the bed, grabbing his pants. He put them on quickly as I wrapped myself in a blanket toga. I followed Mike out to the living room, watching as Mike opened the door.

I was shocked to see Hudson standing there, a small bouquet of purple hyacinths, white roses and succulents. My jaw dropped at the sight, unable to say anything other than, "Uh..."

He looked up, immediately seeing Mike standing in the doorway, still shirtless. His gaze flicked to me briefly, seeing me in nothing but a blanket, before settling back on Mike, who was now standing straight, letting go of the door.

"You Son of a BITCH!" Hudson yelled, dropping the flowers before launching at Mike, swinging a right hook that connected with his nose.

Mike stumbled back with a grunt, grabbing at his nose which was already bleeding. He looked at the blood in his hands before his glare settled back on Hudson. I could see what was about to happen, but couldn't think to say anything. Mike rushed Hudson, tackling him to the ground. They rolled around, each elbowing, kicking, and punching the other.

"Oh for the love of God," I growled, doing my best to get in without losing the carefully place fabric over my body. Hudson had managed to roll on top, and I pulled at his shoulder, yelling, "Get off him!!!"

He shook me off with ease, and I fell on my butt by the door. Glaring at my ex, I grabbed the bouquet and started beating him on his back and head, anywhere I could connect really, as I yelled, "KNOCK IT OFF!!!" With every hit, petals and flowers broke off, littering my floor with floral arrangements.

They slowed, Hudson finally looking at me as I readjusted my blanket. His gaze look sadly defeated with a busted lip and bruising eye. His fist was decorated with Mike's blood. Mike was able to move out from under him, still holding Hudson's flannel checked shirt collar tightly, keeping him at a distance. His other fist was up and ready for any more fighting if Hudson made a move.

I dropped the ruined bouquet, breathing hard from the exertion. "Hudson," I huffed. I pointed to the door. "Go home." He opened his mouth to speak, and I growled, "Go home!"

His mouth snapped shut and he turned to leave. Mike let go of his shirt, watching him as Hudson left silently. I quickly shut the door and locked it just as I saw Hudson turn to say something. Probably another empty apology, but I'd never know, since I closed the door on his face. Deep down, I knew I didn't need to hear it.

I rushed to Mike, who held his rib with a wince. "Are you ok?"

He gave a pained nod. "I will be," he grumbled.

"Good," I breathed. Then I punched his shoulder. "That was really stupid!"

"Ow!" Mike gasped, grabbing his shoulder and shooting me a dirty look. I returned it with my own disapproving glare. "You know he hit me first."

"Yeah," I huffed. "I expect *him* to be stupid. He cheated on *me*." It came out sounding more narcissistic than I meant it, but it was true. "You're supposed to be smarter."

"What? Was I not supposed to defend myself?"

"No, but tackling him wasn't ideal either."

He looked at me carefully, as if reading my innermost thoughts before smirking with his busted lip. "You liked it, didn't you?"

I shrugged nonchalantly as I replied, "I'm not saying he didn't deserve it, but ..." I trailed off as Mike laughed, again wincing, holding his bruising side. I let out a sigh, helping him up as I said, "Come on. Let's get you cleaned up."

I walked him back to my bathroom, dodging petals with every step. I set him against the counter, wetting a small rag and dabbing at every cut.

His green eyes never left me as I worked on him. "Are you ok?" he asked, a hint of worry in his tone.

I gave him a small confused look before going back to tending his wounds. "Why wouldn't I be ok?"

He gave me a look that said I should know the answer to my own question. When I didn't clue in, he said, "That was the first time you've seen him since ..."

He trailed off, and I didn't need him to finish. Since I'd walked in on them. He cleared his throat before adding, "I know it bothers some people, unexpectedly running into an ex who cheated on them."

He was right. It was different than normal. Running into just an ex was like running into an old friend. Running into an ex who had cheated on you was different. Especially if the relationship had been remotely serious. It was like feeling as if I needed to prove I wasn't the wounded one. That maybe he hurt me, but he could never break me. That my life was already so much better without him. There was so much pressure to prove that I wasn't the one holding him back, but that it was him holding me back. It was that, and so many more levels I just couldn't explain.

I didn't want Hudson back. Not ever. With that pressure to prove myself came pain, humiliation, and self-loathing that I was ever stupid enough to trust him.

I gave Mike a bittersweet smile. I loved that he cared that much. I knew I was doing better for myself already. "It's better with you here." He gave me a small, but proud, smile as his fingers found mine, intertwining with them.

I stood on my tip toes and placed a small kiss on his lips, hoping he felt every emotion I was feeling for him in that moment. I felt his other hand run through my hair as he deepened the kiss. Even with the busted lip, his mouth felt like heaven.

I pulled away, smiling. "I believe we were in the middle of something before we were rudely interrupted," I said playfully, letting some of my blanket toga slip, exposing my breast.

I felt his arm go around my waist as he laughed with me, "So, rudely." He let me guide him back to the bed, abandoning the blanket to the bathroom floor.

#InClosing

It was the beginning of Spring semester, and like every return from break, apparently, Mike and his roommates held a big dinner. They had done this every semester since they all moved in together two years ago, and this would be my first time going. And I was really excited.

Over the last couple weeks of the previous semester, I had really gotten to know Jo, her girlfriend Emily, and Kevin. I'd seen Jo and Emily a couple times at pride events I'd attend with Aimee in the past. They didn't go often, but Jo was definitely recognizable.

She had bright pink hair cut short and cutting gray eyes. She had a square jawline and thin lips, but a brilliant smile. She usually wore tight striped t-shirts with a vest and jeans.

Emily was her exact opposite. The Yin to Jo's Yang. She had long brown hair, styled in cascading waves against copper skin. She both looked and dressed like a model, and her make-up was always on point. Emm and I always had fun when I let her play with my make-up.

Kevin was the nerd of the group. He was a chemistry major who had an obsession with videogames and comic books. He was also an amazing chef, which was why he was the designated cook for the first evening back. I helped with sides. Jo and Mike were on drinks, while Emily set the table.

As everyone sat down to eat, Jo lifted up her glass, saying, "To a new semester!' We all clinked our glasses, sharing a laugh as we began to eat. It was just as comfortable as a normal family dinner, full of laughter and jabs.

"So, Rebel," Jo started, a knowing smile on her face as she asked as she finished her plate, "You're going to be joining us for dinner more often, right?"

Mike grabbed my hand, giving me a smile.

"Oh! Please say you will!" Emily cheered. "Mike is so much less of a stick in the mud with you here!" Mike sent her a mock hurt expression, and she stuck her tongue out, clearly in jest.

I squeezed his hand back as I answered, "Well that's the plan."

Emily squealed pulling me into a hug. The night continued as usual. Board games in more drinks until everyone slowly trickled back to their rooms for the evening. Mike grabbed my hand and his green gaze caught my eyes. "Are you staying?"

I smiled, grasping his hand back tightly. I pulled him in for a simple kiss, and that familiar shock ran through me at just the contact. I pulled away, quickly sending a text to Lucy. *Don't wait up. Staying with Mike.*

I looked back at him with an eager smirk, before getting back up, and leading him back to his room.

* ~ * ~ *

"So, what do you think?" Rebel asked, snuggling up next to Mike as he turned the last page of her book.

He gave her a mixed expression, as he dropped her manuscript on the bed. Rebel felt her heart pounding in her chest. "It's not exactly as I remember."

Rebel rolled her eyes. "It was three years ago. Of course it's not going to be exactly like you remember." She looked at him carefully as she asked, "But do you think it's any good?"

He smiled, caressing her cheek before pulling her into a kiss. "It's great," he breathed before kissing her again. "I can send it to my editor if you want."

Rebel smiled, pulling Mike close. "No. This story can stay between us." She pulled him into another kiss. She finally finished a novel. A story. The best love story she knew.

More Books by A. M. H. Johnson

Young Adult

Spiritwalker Series

Midnight Over Moores

Upcoming Novels By A. M. H. Johnson

<u>YA</u>

<u>Spiritwalker Series</u>

Ghosts On Gaston

<u>Romance</u>

<u>Endless Night Series</u>

Night Falls

First Sun [Prequel]

<u>#Hipster</u>
#Hipster: DIL in Training